CW01432945

Enemy

Enemy Aliens

Elizabeth Barr

'... Meanwhile the wild geese, high in the clean blue air,
are heading home again.
Whoever you are, no matter how lonely,
the world offers itself to your imagination,
calls to you like the wild geese, harsh and exciting —
over and over announcing your place
in the family of things.'

                                        Mary Oliver

Copyright © 2016 Elizabeth Barr

The right of Elizabeth Barr to be identified as the Author of the
Work has been asserted by her in accordance with the
Copyright Designs and Patents Act 1988.

First published in Great Britain in 2016
By ER Press
Revised Second Edition 2016

**All rights reserved. No part of this publication may be
reproduced, stored in a retrieval system or transmitted,
in any form or by any means without the prior written
permission of the publisher, nor be otherwise circulated
in any form of binding or cover other than that in which
it is published and without a similar condition be
imposed on the subsequent purchaser.**

ISBN
978-1-326-56596-1

Typeset by ER Press
Printed and bound in Great Britain by
Lulu.com

For all the descendants of
Johann and Ada Gohrt

Author's Note

Our great-grandparents did leave Germany and came to settle in England in the 1870s. My great-grandfather and his son, my grandfather, did subsequently spend the First World War interned at Knockaloe as enemy aliens.

However, this story is not a family history, but a fiction based on how I have imagined their lives might have been. I never met them, or was told anything about them until I was in my teens.

My many cousins would each probably tell this story quite differently, but it is for them that I have tried to picture how life might have been on our shared family tree.

Emil von Ackermann *m.* (Judith Romer)

(Heinrich) (Johann) **Liese** *m.* Ernst Schindler (Kort) (Ludvig) *****Anna** *m.* **Otto Lohmann**

Nicolai **Margarethe** **Hans** *m.*Shirley Leon Eva

(Edward Lohmann *m.* Ruth Mendelsohnn)

Edgar *m.* Greta *****Otto** *m.* **Anna Ackermann** **Trude** *m.* Tom Metcalfe **Clara**

*Anna Ackermann *m.* ***Otto Lohmann**

Wilhelm**   **Alice** *m.* **Gerard Belringer**   **Frederick (Freddie)**   **Emily**

Maisie

** Wilhelm Lohmann (William Logan) *m.* **Leah Jones**

Albert *m.* **Isobel**   **Edgar**   **Leo** *m.* **Martha**   **Philip**   **Molly**   **Clifford**   **Sam** *m.* **Hazel Lancashire**   **Freddy**

Michael **Margo** David   **Mark**   **Alice**

A Photograph Album

The World's End – October 1963

The photograph album had soft black pages, its fading sepia pictures held neatly in place with glued black paper corners. Alice Logan looked up at her brother, who had finished eating and was already looking round to see if there was anyone he knew in the crowded pub. It was nine o'clock. People at the bar waiting for tables stared hopefully at them, and more were still arriving – whenever the door opened she could see it was pitch dark outside.

'So who are they?'

Mark grinned at her and stood up.

'You can have… let's see – five guesses.'

She frowned up at him as he went over to talk to people at the bar. He turned and waved back at her and pointed to the album. She sighed, and began to inspect the photographs. On the front page was an enlarged picture of a plump middle-aged woman with grey hair tied up in a bun. She was sitting upright on a wicker chair in a long linen dress with a high collar pinned with a cameo brooch; leaning with one hand on her chair and looking directly at the camera was a stocky man with a greying beard and long moustache, dressed in a thick tweed suit and waistcoat with a fob watch on a chain hanging from a lower button. They were outside a small house, the coal chute and drain pipes just visible behind two large pot plants artfully placed to conceal them; on dusty ground in front of the couple was laid out a long fur stole.

Alice looked up as a tall girl with long blonde hair wearing what looked like a black ballet tutu over white tights came over to the table.

'Anything else? Pudding? Coffee?'

'Yes, please – coffee for two. My brother will be back in a minute.'

The girl took away their plates. Alice lit a cigarette and propping up the album on her lap against the table, turned the pages with one hand. There was a large wedding group taken outside a civic building, with what appeared to be the same two people standing on either side of the bride and groom; they were also among another family group that included an exceptionally tall young man with either white or very blonde hair, all of them dressed up to the nines and standing on the steps outside another large public building; there were several studio portraits of babies being held out in invisible arms to the camera in long, ornate Christening gowns that reached to the ground; and of a man leaning over the rail of a ship. There was a faded photograph of 20 men standing outside a long hut, all wearing flat caps, apart from one who was bare-headed, and one with a trilby, a boy who only looked about 16-years old. They looked shabby and dusty and as though their clothes had seen better days; but they were grinning cheerfully at the camera.

Alice looked up quickly as her brother came back to their table.

'*Should* I recognise any of them? Who are they? Or were they? These pictures are all very old.'

'Well, I'll tell you. They are all our relations.'

'Really? How come? '

'We need to do some proper research. I want you to help me – better than doing nothing all day.'

'Oh Mark. I'm not doing nothing – I'm thinking.'

Her brother laughed. With her round face, brown eyes and short dark hair cut in a fringe she looked more like twelve than seventeen.

'Well go on. Tell me more about these people. How are they related to us?'

The waitress came over with their coffee and smiled at Mark.

'You ordered coffee?'

'Did I? Oh good – thank you so much.'

Noticing her brother gaze admiringly at the waitress, Alice gave him an exasperated frown. He saw it and grinned back at her.

Alice poured the coffee, and put sugar in for both of them; Mark lit two cigarettes and handed her one. He laughed as Alice continued to look reprovingly at him.

'OK. Well.... The first thing to know is that they are all German.'

He paused to see the effect on her. She looked blank.

'You see this man?' Mark reached across Alice for the album and turned to another picture before handing it back to her. She looked at a faded photograph of a middle-aged man with a moustache and a self-conscious smile walking towards the camera through a town square. He was wearing a trilby hat, a white shirt and tie, and he was holding two books in his leather-gloved hands. Behind him high tiers of stone-faced windows rose up over the shop awnings down a long street receding towards a distant point where she could just make out a tall gothic church spire.

'This was taken by a street photographer – in Dresden in 1931. That's Pa's father.'

'*Dad's* father? Grandfather Will?'

'Yup. Grandfather Will. It's a postcard photograph taken on the third of September 1931. He's written on the back: *On the romp in Dresden.*'

'But ... That's not German. And Grandfather Will *wasn't* German. You knew him.'

'Well – I was only about four when he died. It's all a bit complicated. Do you remember, in the flat in Richmond before we moved to Kent – you were very little, but you might just remember a Mr Belringer, who used to visit Dad sometimes?'

'Was he that old man with very white hair? I sort of do.'

'And do you remember that we had three or four different young German au pair girls who helped Ma while we were living there?'

'Vaguely. I only remember Kali. We got stuck in the lift together one day and she kept screaming until someone came and rescued us.'

'Well I now think all these girls were sent to us by Gerard Belringer, because he would always come to see us when he was on his way to and from Germany. And last week I was up in Manchester to see a chap also called Belringer, Robert Belringer – who works for Granada Television. It's an unusual name and it turns out that Robert is the son of Pa's old friend. And it was Robert who told me that our Grandfather Will was German.'

'And how on earth does he know that?'

'Robert had this album with him to show me, which he'd borrowed from our cousin Margo when he knew he would be seeing me. Margo knows the whole story too.'

'Margo? Now which one is she?'

'Margo is Uncle Leo's daughter. After Grandfather Will died, Grandmother Leah went to live with Margo's family. The album must have belonged to her, and then been put away and forgotten about after she died – until Margo found it.'

Alice looked doubtful. 'It all sounds far too complicated … what makes this Belringer person say Grandfather Will was German?'

'Robert has seen these photographs and it turns out that *his* father – Pa's old friend Gerard Belringer – is in one of them …' Mark paused to make sure she was listening properly '… his own wedding photograph … to one of *our* great-aunts!'

'Golly! So we must be related to Robert Belringer? So *he's* German?'

'No. He isn't.'

'Then who is German? You haven't said anything that makes anybody German yet…. I don't want us to be German.'

'Grandfather Will *was* German. Pa is only half German because Grandmother Leah was Welsh, but Robert told me that

Grandfather Will was interned on the Isle of Man as an "enemy alien" all during the Second World War.'

'No! My God! You don't mean he was a Nazi?'

'No, no. It doesn't necessarily mean that. Even Jews who had managed to escape the Nazis ended up being interned. But he *was* German.'

'Well... then... so why don't we have a German name? Logan isn't German. Is it?'

'The family changed the name. The big picture in the front of the album is of our great grandparents, Otto and Anna *Lohmann*, who came over to Liverpool from Hamburg sometime in the 1870s. Grandfather Will must have only been a baby.'

'Are you quite sure about this?'

'Cousin Margo knows much more than I can tell you. I want you to write to her and ask her. Or better still – go and see her. According to Robert she has all sorts of things, lots of letters and diaries. She can tell you much more.'

'Well it would be more fun than the stupid secretarial course Mum wants me to go on. But I've never even met any of Dad's side of the family. I can't just turn up and start asking lots of questions about being German.'

'Well, at least write to Margo. She knows far more about it than I do. I only know what Robert has told me.' He stood up.

'Anyway, I'm going to pay the bill now and take you back to the flat. I've got an early start.' He got up. 'I'm away filming for the next two weeks, remember. So you can stay up here if you want.'

'Anybody famous?'

'Yes. Do you remember Huw Weldon? He used to present children's TV.'

'Golly yes. Him. I didn't like him. He did *All Your Own* and was patronising to annoying young goody-goodies in school uniform with handicraft hobbies.

Mark went off in search of the waitress while Alice stayed at the table lost in thought. He came back to the table five minutes later.

Come on, Alice. We must go.'

'I was just wondering … I mean why would our great-grandparents have left Germany to come to live here in the first place?'

'I know. It would be really interesting to find out more. Please do some proper research.''

As she stood up to go, Alice said, 'I will. I'll make this my project. It might stop Mum from nagging me for a bit.'

1

Auswanderers

Hamburg, Cuxhaven – 2 May 1875
Passenger lists of emigrants leaving Hamburg on board *P.S. Berlin:*
Otto and Anna Lohmann, Wilhelm Johannis Lohmann (infant), Clara and Trude Lohmann (juveniles).

In the pre-dawn darkness of a cold May morning, Anna Lohmann, carrying a small vanity case, walked through the crowded quay at Cuxhaven and up the gangway of *P.S. Berlin*. It was 5 a.m. and the paddle steamer was already filling up with departing passengers. Otto, a little shorter than his wife, walked beside her, and behind them came his two teenage sisters, Clara and Trude. Clara, the younger, was holding in her arms a sleeping child; Wilhelm's blanket trailed on the ground. They were followed by a porter with their four suitcases.

Reaching the top of the gangway they stopped, unsure where they were to go. The porter put down the two largest cases and pushed passed them. They followed him up another flight of steps. Looking down they could see into the gloom of the deck below where the 'steerage' passengers were crowded in together. The porter led them into a saloon where there were benches and tables. It was lit by gas lamps and already nearly full, largely occupied by a group of forty or fifty young men shouting animatedly to each other above the penetrating hiss of the paddle steamer's engines.

Otto stood still for a moment, listening to their loud voices and laughter. Then he led his family back outside to a wooden bench he had noticed under the steps that led up to the top deck. He himself went down to help the porter bring up the last two cases. The family squeezed up together along the bench with their luggage, too exhausted to speak. Wilhelm was held on his young aunt's lap while Anna lifted the veil on her hat and tried to inspect her face in a compact mirror by the dim light of a small gas lamp above them. Wilhelm started to whimper; Anna held out her arms and Clara passed him to her. Otto found his way to the side of the ship and leant over the rail, smoking a yellow cigarette.

The upper and lower decks of the steamer were crowded with whole families of grandparents, parents, aunts, uncles and young children, hoping to seek their fortune abroad. Mechanisation was enriching industrialists all over Europe, men like Anna's father, Emil von Ackermann, with his large city-based silk and velvet factory. But at the same time it was undermining the home and cottage industries that for centuries had sustained rural life in the Rhineland and Bavaria. A rapidly increasing population combined with rising living costs and taxation meant that traditional small farms, always struggling to subsist, were no longer able to support even one family. Some communities were even offering to pay the passage costs for their poorest members, in exchange for them giving up all citizenship rights and promising never to return.

Travel by train and steamship had become cheaper and easier and relatives and friends who had already migrated were sending home money and positive reports back from England and America to their hometowns and villages across Germany, encouraging others to follow. And Otto knew from his brother's letters how, in England, in the back streets of Liverpool, Manchester, Bradford and London, hundreds of new tenement houses were being built for all the foreigners arriving every week to work in warehouses and factories, many owned by enterprising Germans who had seen how the situation was developing at home.

Bakers and confectioners, boot-makers, butchers, drapers, fruiterers, grocers, hosiers, publicans, tailors, tobacco manufacturers and cigar makers, wine, beer and spirit merchants all with German names; the most beautiful Christmas cards and postcards, the choicest coloured illustrations of books, even playing cards, were now being manufactured in London by

German artists. Hoteliers, manufacturers and merchants of all kinds were waiting with open arms for the German workforce arriving by every boat.

Most of the young men on the higher deck were on their way to learn 'the English way'; young medical students, cadet soldiers, artisans, artists, craftsmen, musicians, sons of wealthy merchants travelling abroad to study or to learn a trade – the Prussian custom of *Wanderschaft.* A hundred years earlier they would have travelled on foot with their knapsacks, or ridden on horseback to far-off towns and cities in search of apprenticeships. Now they were taking trains and boats, crossing land and sea to study in foreign universities. They were all equipped with German-English conversation books and excellent coloured maps of London, Liverpool and New York, for many of them would be travelling on from England to America. They would stay away for two or three years, until called back to the Fatherland to do their military service or to run their family businesses.

There were also among them liberal intellectuals leaving Germany for ideological reasons. Like Otto himself, there were many who did not care for the direction in which Bismarck's newly unified German Empire was moving – away from Enlightenment towards an increasingly industry based, military-led nationalism. No business corporation considered itself a success until it had at least one five-star General on its board of directors.

Otto turned to look at the figure of his wife, sitting lost in thought alone on the bench.

'For us it will not be *Wanderschaft'*, Otto thought to himself, 'we will be *Auswanderers*. We shall move on – we shall live in the new world as free citizens.'

A little before six a vivid golden glow slowly appeared along the skyline as the sun began to rise. The ship's rails were lined with passengers waving their farewells and jumping and craning their necks to get a last glimpse of their homeland. On the quay below, a ray of sun lit up the face of an old porter wheeling a last long wagon loaded with tottering piles of luggage through a noisy throng of families and friends blowing passionate kisses to the departing passengers.

Steam pouring from the whistle suddenly stopped as a deafening roar signalled their imminent departure. The ship left port punctually at seven, ploughing through choppy water as bright sunlight, shining through an early morning shower of rain, lit up the city behind them. Otto and his young sisters were out on the deck and stood there together for a long time, watching the receding coast of Germany, the wind slapping the girls' long hair across their faces as they waved goodbye althhough there was nobody there to see them go; Anna remained alone on the bench, her child on her lap. She leaned across for her bag and found a notebook.

'This is the point where your father's view and mine chiefly diverge, Anna,' Otto, coming back from the rail, stood with his legs a little apart, bracing himself against the ship's turbulence. Anna said nothing, but looked up from the wriggling child in her arms to Otto's face, and then back to Wilhelm, who smiled up at her.

'Your father would say that Wanderschaft is good for young men, to travel abroad in order to return home a year or two later, enriched with their new-found skills and knowledge, to benefit the Fatherland. But we are not leaving in order to return as cogs in the national wheels. We are Auswanderers now. We are leaving...' Otto paused and took a deep breath to savour his new idea, '...to be become free citizens of the world!'

Anna frowned doubtfully.

'Anna! Believe me! All will be well. We are moving forwards, not back.'

Anna looked down at Wilhelm again. Then she looked up and smiled.

'Yes, Otto. I believe you. But I hope we free citizens of the world can find some good German breakfast soon.'

He remained still lost in his own thought for a moment, then,

'I will go and see.'

She continued to sit on the bench, quite still. The child moaned and stretched out a long foot under his blanket. She bent down to give him a kiss, then handed him to Clara, who had come back from the rails. Anna picked up her notebook, found her pencil and wrote in it 'Auswanderers'.

Otto made his way through the ship until he eventually found a noisy crowd queuing for the fruhstuckbufett. He returned to his family.

'I am afraid there will be a very long wait. Did anyone bring anything we could eat here?' He looked at his two young sisters.

'I brought a little apfelstrudel for Wilhelm,' said Trude, at fifteen the elder.

'And I have some bonbons,' Clara produced a handkerchief with some sticky looking sweets in it. The all looked at them doubtfully.

'I think we must go and wait in the queue.'

'Will it be all right to leave our luggage here?' Clara asked.

'Push the cases behind the bench so they are not conspicuous.'

Anna looked up quickly. 'But I want them to be conspicuous. I don't want other people to steal our bench. There is nowhere else where we can sit together quietly.'

Trude said, 'Clara and I will stay here and guard. We don't mind.'

'No, no, we must all go. No-one will steal our bench, and anyway we must all go up on deck later and look out for our new country. Give me Wilhelm, Clara. Come along now, this way.'

They trailed after Otto in single file through the crowded saloon and joined the queue at the far end. They stood together silently, and Anna let out an involuntary sigh.

Otto smiled at her. 'We will go outside after this and breathe in some good sea air. Look, look, look. People are leaving. There will soon be room for us.'

An hour later they were sitting at a table in the fruhstuckbufett drinking strong black coffee and eating bread and sausage. The thumps and groans of the paddle steamer made conversation impossible, every word drowned in the roar of the ship's pro-gress. Wilhelm was awake, staring around wide-eyed as Otto held him on his lap and shared small pieces of sausage with him. Clara went over to help an anxious-looking young couple at another table whose three small children were all crying.

Anna suddenly felt faint. She closed her eyes.

*

She was back at home. Her father was saying, 'But Anna! Otto Lohmann is a penniless Jew from Hamburg! Hermann is an old friend of ours, and a national hero! Hermann will marry you, Anna, with my blessing, and with the Baron's blessing.'

She was screaming at him, just as Hermann and his companion came into the room, 'NEVER! He is a cruel bully! You are a cruel bully!'

Then she was whirling from the room. In the sanctuary of her own room, she began laying out clothes on her bed. The loud masculine voices down below panicked her and she began to circle her room, seizing things wildly, scarves, her favourite shoes, her old doll…. As more and more things were heaped up on the bed, she found she couldn't make any sensible decisions. She tried to balance her music sheets on top of a now ridiculous pile of possessions. As the sheet music slid to the floor and spread itself all over the room, she crawled under the tottering pile of clothes into bed, still in her long silk evening dress, and fell into an exhausted, tearful sleep…

*

Anna found she was trembling uncontrollably. She heard Otto's voice saying above the din, '…all go up on deck now…. Trude, get Clara and take Wilhelm up to the top deck. We'll come and find you. If we can't find each other, we'll all meet back at the bench where the cases are.'

The two girls left with Wilhelm, and all three children turned and waved at Otto and Anna from the doorway. Otto smiled and waved back but made no move to stand up. He looked at Anna for a moment then he leaned closer so he could say in her ear, 'Anna? Anna? Are you all right?'

Her shaking slowly stopped. She gave a big sigh and shook her head. 'I'm sorry. I just felt a bit sick for a moment. It's the awful motion. I'm all right now, Otto. Let's follow the children.'

He helped her out of her seat and they went up to the top deck to look for Trude and Clara and Wilhelm. They found them standing by the rail at the stern, watching a line of seagulls gliding along behind them above the wake. Anna stared over their heads across the miles of waves that lay between her and her vanished homeland. Then she turned to Otto. 'Can we go back to the bench now?'

When he saw she was settled and clearly wanted to be left on her own there, Otto said, 'I won't be far away, Anna,' and made his way back to the rail. After he had gone, Anna took the notebook and pencil out of her bag and wrote, 'Auf Wiedersehen.'

Much later Otto came to find her and they went up to the top deck together. The evening sky was dark grey and a light rain beginning to fall. Passengers were shouting to one another as, in the far distance, lights on the East coast of England could just be seen. Everyone crowded forwards to stare at the approaching land. The ship lurched as the hissing paddle steamer engines suddenly slowed and fell silent, passengers were flung unsteadily into one another; after a few shrieks there was laughter. Otto and Anna hung on to each other and she looked around for Wilhelm and the girls.

High over their heads they heard another sound. Faint at first, then much louder. A flying V formation of geese suddenly appeared from nowhere, overtaking the ship. Then another. Then another. People began shouting to each other '*Schauen!* Look!' as dozens of skeins of sixty or seventy geese, their wings creaking, flew over their heads, calling out to each other with high, wailing cries. The first formations broke up and the birds began to plunge and wheel and somersault crazily down to the shore a few miles ahead of them. Then the next. Then the next. Anna looked around again and to her relief could see Trude holding Wilhelm up in the air so he could see over the heads of the other passengers. Clara was with them, leaping up and down with excitement.

Clara called out to Anna, 'Look! *Auswanderers*, Anna! Like us!'

Standing unsteadily, holding on to Otto in the middle of the noisy, surging crowd, looking at the plunging geese, the grey sea and the rain soaked land ahead, Anna said, 'Yes, Clara. Just like us.'

2

Citizens of the World

Hull – 2 May 1875

The paddle steamer disembarked at the Port of Hull that evening; steerage passengers remained on board until the weekly 'migrant' train would take them across to Liverpool. Nobody was allowed into the city itself because of fear of the spread of tuberculosis, which the local population were convinced German immigrants carried. Otto and his family, and all the passengers with approved papers and confirmed destinations, were allowed into the Port's waiting area where they could wash and shower before making their way on foot to Hull station to spend the night in the railway hotel.

Liverpool – 3 May 1875

At 11a.m. the following morning the Lancashire and Yorkshire link railway carried them the four-hour journey across the Pennines to Liverpool. Anna sat silently staring out of the window for most of the journey, and Trude and Clara left her in peace while they gazed at the scenery and Otto made them practise their English as they pointed out the sights to each other.

Otto's elder brother, Edgar, who had been living in England for the last two years training to become an architect, met them at the station and ordered a cab to take them to where he had organised lodgings for them in the promising sounding St Martin's Cottages. He had bought some basic provisions for them – milk and bread, some rusks for the baby, and ham and tomatoes for their supper.

St Martin's Cottages turned out to be two bleak, gas-lit tenement blocks of over a hundred flats and maisonettes. Their own flat consisted of two bedrooms, each furnished with two single beds, plus a living room with gas lamps and a coal fire and oven, which Edgar had already lit, so the flat felt warm. There was no bathroom, but there were WCs on the landings of the open staircases, and inside the flat there was a six-foot-long scullery with running water and a sink where they could wash themselves and do the laundry. There was one big table in the sitting room with four chairs, and a high-chair for Wilhelm that Edgar had made himself.

As soon as they opened the front door to their new home, Anna could smell damp. She began sniffing suspiciously and stalking around the flat peering hard at the walls and ceiling until she discovered a brown stain on the ceiling of the scullery. She pointed to it dramatically. Edgar, whose own firm had built the tenement, said, 'I'm so sorry, Anna. Yes, there is a small leak coming from upstairs. I noticed it this morning. I have arranged for someone to mend it for you.'

While Anna settled Wilhelm in his high-chair and gave him the milk and rusks, the two girls began unpacking. Edgar and Otto went out for a walk together.

'So you decided I wasn't mad to come to England?'

'No Edgar – I never thought that. I often wanted to come myself. But then – well, you know what happened. I hoped for a time that in the end Anna's father might come to accept me as her husband. We had some interesting conversations when I was round at their house teaching Anna to play the piano. Poor Anna has had to give up so much by marrying me. But it became clear he would never forgive her. I knew I could never make her life in Germany as comfortable and secure as she had been accustomed to, and when our own dear mother died, I felt that now was the right time to see if we wouldn't both be happier starting our life together in a different country. Anna has been so very hurt.'

'Well it is a great pleasure for me – I have missed you and I am very happy you have all been able to come.'

'I didn't feel I could abandon our young sisters in Hamburg with their Aunt – so – here we all are! It was very good of you to find the flat for us, Edgar. Although it is a bit....'

'I know. I know. I am sorry. I had hoped that I would have finished our own home by the time you arrived, but... I can't afford to pay anyone to help me, and it is a big project. I am enjoying myself though. You will be able to help me now you are here and as soon as it is finished, of course, there will be room for both our families. Greta and I are both looking forward to that.'

'We are all very grateful to you, Edgar, and to Greta. As for Trude and Clara – this is all one big adventure for them at the moment.'

'They can start by coming to stay at our house for a few days while you and Anna get yourself settled in here. You will be going straight down to the Council offices tomorrow, I suppose?'

'Yes. I have an appointment to see my Head of Department in the morning, and I expect to be set straight to work. On the boat coming over I had this idea, Edgar. We are not going to think of ourselves as poor migrant Germans. We are going to think of ourselves as "citizens of the world"!'

'Good, Otto. I think that our future, too, lies here. There are many opportunities, and for you especially. I've come to realise that music is such an important part of life for people living here. Whenever I am drawing up the plans for a new home, the architect has always included a 'music room'. So I believe there will be plenty of work for you to do.'

'My God – whatever is that smell?'

'Ah! I am afraid that comes from a bone-manure works across the canal. It's not always quite so bad. It does come and go....'

'It's foul! Anna will be appalled. But – I dare say we shall get used to it. We'd better get back now and see how Anna and the girls are getting on.'

Anna had managed to store most of their clothes in the small wardrobe and chest of drawers in the bedrooms, and the rest in the small case the girls were taking with them to stay with Edgar and his wife. Trude and Clara had put out plates with bread and ham on the table, boiled a kettle and made tea by the time the two men returned. After they had eaten, Edgar took his two young sisters away with him on the horse-tram – much to their delight – which went as far as the Tithebarn Street railway Exchange station in the city centre. From there they made their way on foot to begin their holiday at Edgar's new home.

Anna wrote in her notebook that night. *'Edgar has moved us all into a damp, smelly hovel!'*

The next morning, Otto took the tram into the city centre. Soon after he had left, a man from the Council arrived at the Cottages to investigate the damp patch. Without Trude and Clara to help her, Anna panicked and addressed him in a rapid gabble of German and English exclamations of shock and despair, pointing dramatically to the stain and waving her arms in the air to indicate the smell. The man stood and stared at her for a few moments before going away without saying a word.

Two days later Edgar came back with another plumber, who fixed the leak and painted over the stain. By then Anna had experienced the even fouler stink coming from the bone-manure works nearby and her next diary entry was incandescent. *'How dare the English suggest that we Germans are the unclean ones?'*

Once the girls returned from visiting their uncle, Trude found work with a nearby local family who needed a live-in housemaid. She came home one day a week, full of well-observed stories about the strange ways of middle-class English family life that always astounded Anna. Clara stayed on in the flat, helping Anna and sharing the smaller bedroom with Wilhelm. Otto brought home a second-hand sewing machine, and Anna and Clara sewed new curtains for all the windows.

Many of the other tenants were also German immigrants. There was a constant cry of 'Speak English!' out of the windows by parents to their children, playing and chattering to each other in the street below. Other families were mainly from Ireland and had left their own country with similar stories to the Germans, of unemployment and small-holdings and rural cottage industries no longer able to sustain family life. Friendships quickly formed, particularly among the children, and soon the Lohmanns, the Vogels and the Gohrts were on easy terms with their neighbours, the O'Briens, the Irwins, the McCaffreys and the Currivans.

Anna began to explore the neighbourhood and found to her delight a nearby market where she could buy honeycomb and fresh eggs, and even milk from a farmer who sent a few cows into the city for milking early each morning. For Anna, looking after the flat meant an unfamiliar amount of drudgery that exhausted her, especially washing days, but she knew how a good home should be run, and with Clara's help kept everything aired, dusted and polished, the windows bright, the paintwork distempered, and fresh flowers always on the parlour table.

'We had a big washing for two days. I am tired, Oh, so very tired.'

Anna's diary, 18 July 1875

Over the next few years, Otto's energy and enthusiasm for their new life infected them all. He found Edgar was right – the Liverpool Council had plenty of work for him maintaining the pianos and harpsichords in all the public civic buildings as well as in the local schools.

Since the Great Exhibition, American-style pianos were being mass-produced and sold in Europe. In Liverpool more and more people wanted their children to be taught to play because they could now afford to have an upright piano in their own homes. Schools began to acquire them for their classrooms, too, so that inexperienced children wouldn't be learning on concert grand pianos. There was a shortage of piano teachers, and before long Otto was being asked to give lessons at the school as well as maintaining all the Council instruments. His reputation as a teacher grew, and he was asked to give private piano lessons to some of the parents of the children he taught at school.

Otto made friends easily and loved the spirit of Liverpool people. He persuaded a teacher from the Council to come once a week to help them all improve their English in exchange for teaching her to play the piano. Their German neighbours were all invited to bring their children and everyone squeezed into the small parlour.

*

West Derby, Liverpool – 1880

In 1880, much to Anna's relief, they were able to move into the other half of Edgar's new house in West Derby. It meant that Otto could have a piano in his own home. Edgar qualified as an architect and three years later he and his family left Liverpool and moved down to Exeter, where he had been offered a junior partnership in a big southern firm.

For the next few years Otto and Anna stayed on in the West Derby house, paying rent to Edgar. Otto and Anna's eldest daughter, Alice, was born there in 1884. Another pregnancy ended in miscarriage, but in 1887 Wilhelm's brother Frederick was born.

Later that year, Edgar wrote to tell Otto that he needed to sell the West Derby house as he was building a new family home in Devon, so Otto and Anna moved into a rented de-tached cottage in Boundary Lane.

*

Boundary Lane, Liverpool – 1888

The road outside Otto and Anna's new house was thronged with onlookers the day a horse-drawn pantechnicon drew up outside their door and an upright Broadwood piano was man-handled in through the parlour window – the first piano ever seen in Boundary Lane. Otto could now teach his pupils in his own home. Clara continued to live with them to help Anna with the children, and Trude still shared her room whenever she came home on her days off.

When they had been living in the Cottages Trude had always enjoyed visiting the Anfield market with Anna. On those early visits Trude had met Tom Metcalfe, a Yorkshire 'cow-keeper'. Tom worked for a farmer in outlying Toxteth, and would arrive early every morning at St Martin's Market, bringing a few cows with him for milking. Trude had begun to get to know Tom, and liked him. She was still regularly visiting the market for the family she worked for after she had shown the cook some of the fresh produce she could buy there.

Tom and Trude had begun courting, and in 1889 were married quietly in St Margaret's, Anfield, with Clara as matron of honour. Edgar and Greta came back to Liverpool for the wedding and Otto gave his sister away.

A year later, Tom and Trude left Liverpool and went to live on a farm in the borders of Scotland. She wrote regular news bulletins home to Anna, who was once more shocked and delighted by Trude's acute observations of other people's 'strange ways' – this time it was the habits of the Scots. Edgar reported to Otto that he too heard from Tom from time to time, usually asking for 'a little financial help!

Later that year, Anna gave birth to a second daughter, Emily. She had been very sick during most of her last pregnancy and after a long and exhausting delivery was told that she must have no more children.

My dear Sister,

Greetings!! A great day has dawned! Another letter from you! Congratulations on the birth of another beautiful daughter. I hope you are feeling much better now.

We are all very well. Nicolai has grown very tall. He is a cadet soldier and we are now certain he will have a great career in the cavalry. My son the general! He wants to be just like his 'uncle' Hermann, of course, who is a hero to both our sons. Dear Margarethe has just celebrated her sixteenth birthday, so she is now very grown up, and so very bossy! Even to our little Eva, who is really always as good as gold! Father is working very hard, and Hermann von T has just joined his Board in place of the old Baron. As for me – you will be very proud of me, Anna – I have been elected President of our Berlin Ladies' Guild and will have to make a speech at the next meeting! I am going to say that we should try to become more like the ladies in England - where they have a Queen in charge –

and where I know from my good sister they are respected and listened to far more than we are here

Please send us your own good English news again, Anina - before TOO LONG! Father pretends he is not interested, but I know he 'steals' your letters to read privately when I am not there! We all miss you.

Your affectionate sister,

Liese

Letter from Anna's sister Liese to Anna, 1891

3

'*Arias und Konzertmusik!*'

Liverpool – 1890

Anna remained German in her heart, and as soon as they were old enough, she taught her children to play and sing all the old German folk songs she had loved when she was growing up.

Wilhelm was a gentle rather dreamy young man with no clear idea of where his talents lay. He loved reading, but he had no ambition to do anything in particular. He left school at fourteen and went to work as an assistant to a local pawnbroker. At seventeen, he seemed suddenly to have begun to take a more serious interest in music, accompanying his father to concerts and asking his mother to help him play and sing some of the more difficult pieces she had taught them. This new enthusiasm and diligence was unexpected, and slightly worried Anna. The reason for it only became clear a few months later, when he told them he was thinking of auditioning for the Mossley Hill Choral Society.

'Whatever is he thinking about?' Anna was uneasy – it was so unlike the vague Wilhelm she knew and loved. 'I don't want him hurt.'

'Let us just celebrate, my dear. At last our son is taking an interest in something that will require some effort to achieve.'

In1890 the Mossley Hill Choral Society was the biggest mixed amateur choir in the city, putting on major performances all through the year; their annual performance of the Messiah each Christmas was so popular that it was impossible to get seats unless you booked a year in advance. The auditions to become a member were as competitive and daunting as for any professional choir, and the Society was acquiring an international reputation. They had travelled to Heidelberg, Salzburg and the Crystal Palace in London to take part in the great music festivals, and renowned singers from Europe sometimes came along to sing in the Society's own Oratorio performances in Liverpool. It would be a great challenge for Wilhelm to be able to join them.

Otto had a friend whose company designed the programmes for the Choral Society. Harry Rea was Irish and he too had begun life in Liverpool in one of the tenements, but was now doing very well in business. His son, Tommy, had been one of Otto's first piano students at the school, but since he had shown very little aptitude or enthusiasm, Harry decided he might as well take the lessons himself as he'd already paid for them. This arrangement had gone on for several years, long after

Tommy had left home and found work as a salesman, and the two older men had become firm friends.

Otto discussed with Harry his own and Anna's surprise at Wilhelm's ambition to join Mossley Hill.

'Ah well now, Otto. You mustn't be surprised about that at all. Isn't the Mossley Hill Choral Society just the great place for young men and women to meet one another? I wouldn't be at all surprised if that were not young Will's reasoning. And if he can get in, it will be a great thing for him surely.'

'But Wilhelm already has many friends,' Anna objected when Otto reported Harry's opinion back to her. 'Why would he need to make more?'

'He doesn't know many girls. His sisters' friends are all too young.'

'Oh Otto! He's only a lad.'

'He's seventeen, Anna. But you shouldn't worry. It is very unlikely they will accept him, and it won't do him any harm to have to work hard for something for a change.'

Wilhelm, much to everyone's surprise, and after much perseverance, was finally admitted to the prestigious choir on his nineteenth birthday in April 1893.

'A great day has dawned!' Anna wrote in her diary. *'My son sings in a famous choir!'*

*

'Hallo.' As soon as she saw him, on his first day as a new member of the Choral Society, Leah Jones noticed the warm, twinkling brown eyes, floppy brown hair and big banana smile that Wilhelm bestowed with shy warmth on anyone who spoke to him. It wasn't exactly love at first sight, more a feeling of recognising someone she felt she had always known. There he was, and she just knew he was the one for her. Like his father, Wilhelm was not very tall, five foot seven, and Leah, who was tall for a girl, stood a good half an inch higher, but neither of them minded the difference. For Wilhelm it was an instant attraction. He especially loved her beautiful large, dark eyes, her grave manner and her musical Welsh accent.

At twenty-two, Welsh-born Leah had a clear mezzo-soprano voice, and was a rising star at Mossley Hill. When she was eleven, Leah's family had been forced to leave Wales when their valley home was flooded to build a reservoir to supply water for English cities, including Liverpool. Six villages all now lay under water; the water company had given the villagers the choice of accepting a sum of money in compensation or of being re-housed in Liverpool. There were eight children, Leah being the only daughter, and her father, a cooper by trade, thought he stood a better chance of finding employment in the big English city than in Wales. So they had all moved to Liverpool.

Soon after they arrived, their mother had contracted typhoid, and died, as did the youngest child, Gareth, a four-month-old baby. Leah became a little mother to the rest of her brothers, but for her father, the death of his wife, life in the strange city and the problems of finding a job were too much for him and he began drinking heavily. There was not enough money to feed them all, and eventually all the children were taken to live in the Poor House. Her father died two years later, and at the age of fourteen, Leah was found a position in service as a maid in a big house. She was never to get over her anger and regret that she hadn't been able to look after her younger brothers and keep them all at home. It would make her one day a fiercely protective mother to her own sons and the terror of her future daughters-in-law.

The family who employed the young Leah discovered that she had a beautiful singing voice, and had encouraged her to join the local church choir. They in turn had helped prepare her for her audition to the Mossley Hill choir when she was seventeen.

*

When Wilhelm joined them, the Mossley Hill choir were just beginning rehearsals for a summer time concert in Princes Park; the grand finale was to be a chorale performance of Purcell's *Dido and Aeneas*. Leah was understudying the part of

Dido, as well as singing a comedy duet about a lovelorn *valet de chambre.*

From the start, Leah and Wilhelm were always together. He learned the parts of Aeneas and Belinda so that she could rehearse with him. All that summer they would go for long cycle rides out into the countryside and would sit in the empty, echoing hills, singing together all afternoon, loudly and happily. Leah prepared picnics for them which Wilhelm carried in his rucksack.

Although she was a strikingly good-looking girl, Leah had always put off any would-be suitors by her stiff, shy manner. Having had so much to do with looking after her younger brothers, and then going into service where the two other members of staff were both much older, she had never learned how to make light conversation with people her own age. She was also not inclined to be charmed by anyone who might want to dominate her. The one thing Leah had learned from her childhood experience was that she must keep control over her own destiny. Other people let you down.

*

Liverpool – 1898

Wilhelm was earning very little. He left the pawn-brokers and took a job as a clerk in an estate agent's office. He was still living at home and began saving hard, but it was not for another five years, on his 24th birthday in April 1898, that Wilhelm and Leah were married in Leah's Baptist church. All the Mossley Hill choir members were invited, and the singing was spectacular. Anna and Otto paid for the reception held in the church hall, which took the form of a concert party.

'My son a married man! But how beautiful it all was! No speeches – just arias and Konzertmusik!'

Anna's diary, 1 April 1898

4

Belringer

Liverpool – July, 1900

In the summer of 1900 members of the Mossley Hill choir, including Wilhelm and Leah, were performing a concert of songs and anthems by the now famous English composer Edward Elgar, in the elegant surroundings of St George's Hall Golden Concert Room in Liverpool. It was a prestigious event and all the members of Wilhelm's family were in the audience. During the interval Frederick wandered off back-stage to see if he could find Wilhelm, while most of the audience, including Anna and Otto, drifted outside to enjoy the sunset.

'Professor Lohmann? I believe you teach the piano to a friend of mine – Harry Rea?'

Otto looked round in surprise at the young man speaking to him. 'Yes, yes, Harry is an old friend of ours … er?'

The stranger appeared to be in his early thirties, elegantly dressed in a dark silk dinner suit with a red rose in his button-hole. He laughed and shook Otto by the hand.

'Belringer. Shipping. Harry Rea tells me you are a great musician, Professor.'

'Well! That is very kind of Harry. Is he here tonight? I assure you I am just a humble piano tuner who teaches a little.'

Anna and the two girls, who had edged a little away, were trying to appear as though they were talking animatedly to each other, while Anna strained to catch what Otto and the stranger were saying, 'Would you do me the honour of introducing me to your family, Professor?'

'Well ... yes. Of course. Anna, my dear, this is Mr Belringer. He is a friend of Harry Rea.'

Anna came over to them, looking bemused but smiling politely. 'Is Harry here? I do hope you are enjoying the concert Mr Belringer. Our son and daughter-in-law are both singing in the choir.'

Gerard Belringer congratulated her, agreeing heartily, 'It is certainly a wonderful occasion!'

Otto continued with his introductions, 'Well, these are our other children – this is my eldest daughter, Alice, and her younger sister, Emily. Girls – please say hello to Mr Belringer.' Otto smiled at his daughters and took hold of Emily's hand because she had turned bright pink. Gerard Belringer smiled back at them each in turn and they looked back at him with shy, serious faces. Now sixteen, Alice had grown into a tall, fair haired young woman, strikingly attractive, with slanting green eyes. Gerard Belringer surprised her by suddenly

reaching out to take her hand and looking at her closely, saying, 'You know, you have a fascinating face, Alice!'

Alice blushed and looked helplessly at eleven-year-old,
Emily, who looked back at her with bright eyes, giggled and
blushed even more.

Otto went on hurriedly, '... and here is my beautiful daughter-in-law, Leah, and my elder son Wilhelm and ... now
where's Freddie got to? Well, never mind. My dears – this is
Mr Belringer.'

'It's an honour to meet two members of this renowned
choir. And as one of its sponsors, I am delighted to see a full
auditorium for Elgar's music.'

The stranger took a card from his breast pocket and handed
it to Otto. 'Would you do me the honour, Sir, of bringing your
family to dine with me one day? May I send you an invitation?
Harry will tell me where I can reach you.'

Otto looked at his wife and family who were now all, including Freddie, standing in a row in the evening sunshine with
their mouths slightly open, then he shook his head in bewil-
derment saying, 'Well, we would be very honoured, of course.
It would be a great pleasure. But as you see, we are rather a
large crowd. I don't think we can possibly impose on you.'

'No, no – no imposition. The pleasure will be all mine, I
assure you.'

At that moment a man came out ringing a bell to end the interval, and as they went inside Gerard Belringer bowed gravely to them all, and returned to his seat upstairs in the golden gallery.

*

One week later, Gerard Belringer's invitation arrived – a photograph of a steamer, *RMS Atlantica*, with his name and address printed on the back:

'*Gerard Belringer cordially invites ... for luncheon on his yacht, SS Regina.*' In his own hand he had inserted '*Professor Otto Lohmann and family*' and the date. Underneath he had written: '*My man will meet you at the dock gates and escort you here. G.*'

When Otto spoke to Harry Rea about this strange encounter, he asked him if he knew why Belringer had approached him. Harry told Otto how he and his wife had been sitting next to Gerard in the gallery and had seen Otto and the family arriving down below in the stalls. 'You should know that your eldest daughter has grown into an unusually beautiful young lady, Otto.'

'But who *is* he, Harry? You've never mentioned him to me before. Whatever can he want from me?'

'Ah well now, Otto. This Belringer fellow is something of a man of mystery even to me – and I'm on the local Council these days, remember, so I know everyone! All anyone really knows about him is that he is a young self-made businessman who works in shipping – his company is based here and they build and export parts for ships' engines or some such business – and he travels abroad a lot. I've seen his name above pieces about Europe in the *Manchester Guardian* from time to time, and I've heard rumours that he is an unofficial diplomat behind the scenes. I know he's a Liberal and I hear little snippets about him at our meetings which suggest he knows everyone and goes everywhere. He is a charmer, wouldn't you say, Otto my old friend?'

Harry told Otto he had pointed him and his family out to Gerard as they arrived 'including your beautiful daughter re-member, Otto!' and told him about this wonderful German Pro-fessor who had taught him to play the piano. Gerard had then asked Harry if he would introduce him to them during the in-terval. Unfortunately, as soon as the first half ended Harry's wife had felt faint, and he had had to take her home.

'But I'm glad he made himself known to you, Otto. Perhaps he wants to add to his talents. I told him that if he was thinking of taking up the old piano lessons, he wouldn't find a better professor to teach him in this world or the next!'

*

The yacht was moored at Birkenhead. It was an American-built ocean-going three-masted schooner, with the interior fitted out for conferences and entertaining visitors and just enough space in the hold for a small amount of cargo. For his luncheon party Belringer had invited Harry Rea and his wife as well as Otto and his family. Leah had excused herself because she and Wilhelm had lost their first baby, and now she was expecting her second but was not feeling well. Uniformed waiters served lunch in the saloon to the party of nine on a long elm table that could have seated forty, laid with white linen napkins, porcelain plates, crystal glass and silver cutlery.

Otto was soon privately agreeing with Harry's hint that it was the beauty of his daughter Alice that was the likely reason for this sudden display of interest in his family. Gerard had managed to detach Alice from the party for a personally guided tour of the yacht soon after they arrived, and when he arranged for Anna to be seated on his right, with Alice on his left rather than Harry's wife, who he seated next to Otto at the far end of the table, it confirmed his suspicions.

Belringer was an animated host and regaled his guests with a flow of amusing anecdotes, often told against himself, mainly about famous people he had met, including an account of a recent occasion when he had been sent for by 'a very senior member' of the Liberal Party. There was to be a general election in a couple of months' time and some party members who wanted to maintain the Gladstone tradition of patronage were resisting this man's reforming ideas.

'Now I knew this man to be a modernist, which I am all for, and I supposed – or rather hoped – it was my advice on how to present new Liberal ideas to the electorate that I was being asked for – so I gave it to him – at some length! When I had finished more or less telling him how to run the country, he said, "Er. Thank you, Mr Belringer. That was all very interesting." There was a slight pause, and then he cleared his throat and said, "Um – the reason I asked to see you is … was … I really just hoped you could help me with some shipping figures." I felt such a fool!'

Harry Rea and his wife laughed heartily and cried, 'Good old Gerard!' while Otto and Anna both looked bemused. The young people, encouraged by Gerard Belringer's own loud laughter, began laughing too, and Otto and Anna soon found themselves joining in with everyone else. Afterwards Anna said to Otto, 'I shall never understand the English sense of humour.'

*

Over the next few months there were two further invitations from Gerard Belringer. On one occasion the yacht set sail for the Isle of Man very early one morning with Otto, Anna, Alice,

Emily and Freddie as the only guests, and they had their lunch moored in Douglas harbour.

Another invitation was for Otto, Anna and Alice to attend a very grand and formal lunch party where the 40 guests included journalists and several well-known politicians, including Mr H. H. Asquith, who it turned out was the 'very senior member of the Liberal party' Gerard had talked about on the first occasion. In spite of the rather embarrassing debacle of their first encounter, the Chancellor had been paying attention to Gerard's ideas and had begun to send for him to discuss Liberal Party public relations matters.

All these outings on the yacht were of a style and luxury none of them had ever experienced before, but Otto also realised that there was a shrewd mind behind the cheerful bonhomie of his generous host.

Gerard had begun to call round at their home quite frequently. Sometimes there would be a gap of several weeks, but then he would appear two or three times in a week, usually arriving just after they'd had their supper. He was very relaxed and lively in their company, as he sat smoking his cigar and drinking the whiskey Otto now always had ready to offer him. Emily and Freddie enjoyed his stories and gave each other secret signs of approval, while Alice would laugh a lot, and try to join in.

At other times Gerard would sit talking quietly to Otto in the small parlour while the young were singing and playing the piano in the music room. The two men became good friends. Otto enjoyed their conversations. Often they would discuss Germany and what people had felt about Bismarck.

'I must say, I was very sad when he died, Otto. I always believed Bismarck was a liberal at heart. He introduced many improvements for the lives of Germany's working men. I am hoping our Liberals here will adopt some of his reforming ideas.'

'He may have been a liberal at heart, Gerard, but he was still a Prussian. It is true that he helped create a sort of peace and prosperity in Germany – but only through the threat of a Prussian sword.'

'They have someone far worse in charge now.'

One evening Gerard mentioned the name of Baron von Treitschke, who had been one of Bismarck's advisers and now worked for the Kaiser, and was reported in the British press as being about to make a visit to England. Anna, who had been sitting with them doing her sewing, exclaimed loudly, 'Oh!' Otto smiled at his wife, and began to explain to Gerard that the Baron had been a good friend of Anna's father, Emil, when Anna burst out, 'Yes! Yes! He … and Hermann. No, no. He is not coming here also?'

'I know Baron von Treitschke and his famous son, the General, by reputation only, and have not yet had the pleasure of meeting them. But if they are friends of your family, perhaps they will be calling ...?' Anna looked horrified and Otto shook his head warningly, and the subject was dropped.

Towards the end of these visits Gerard would often look towards Alice, who would join them in the parlour after Emily and Freddie had gone up to their own rooms. He would usually have a piece of news or gossip he had kept especially for her, so their conversation would lead to it seeming quite natural for them to go outside together and walk round the streets arm in arm for a short while before he took his leave. Otto and Anna would both give a big sigh and slowly get up to follow them a little distance behind, also arm in arm. Alice told Freddie and Emily that Gerard had said to her on one of these walks that he was hoping to become Mayor of Liverpool one day, and they had both giggled at the idea.

'Does that mean he will be a lord and you a lady?' Frederick asked her.

'Don't be silly, Freddie.'

*

Over the next two years they gradually began to see Gerard less frequently; he was spending more time than ever abroad, when he wasn't touring the country with Mr Asquith. Like

Gerard, Mr Asquith enjoyed a good drink while they were discussing their strategy. They both agreed that it stimulated the brain. Gerard told Otto he was encouraging 'H.H.' to be seen more in public, listening directly to people's problems, answering their questions and generally appearing to be someone who was open and understood the needs of working people, not just the economy at large.

Gerard occasionally held weekend house parties for journalists and politicians in his home in West Derby, and Alice accepted several invitations to be there and act as hostess. Anna became increasingly concerned that Belringer was monopolising Alice without having any serious intention of proposing to her.

'She is still very young,' Otto said.

'But it's been so long now! And what is his reason for wanting to see her so much and yet saying nothing? What does he intend? You must ask him, Otto. You are her father.'

'But, my dear, Gerard has important work to do, and perhaps does not feel he is in a position to take on the responsibilities of a very young wife.'

'Oh! You men and your important work! And is our daughter's happiness not important?'

It was clear to Anna that Alice was very much in love with Gerard, and it saddened her every time she saw her daughter's beautiful face light up when she saw him or heard that he was coming, and fall again when he left.

*

Liverpool – 1904

In 1904, Anna's elder sister, Liese Schindler, and her ten-year-old son, Hans, came to stay with them in Liverpool while her husband was in London on business. Alice, Freddie and Emily entertained young Hans and taught him to pronounce English words with a Liverpool accent.

Otto was happy to leave Anna and her sister closeted together exchanging all their family news. Liese told Anna that their father, Emil, had sold the family house now and was living with her family.

'He realises he is an old man now he's in his eighties. And although he still goes to the office every day, I know he is lonely. Oh, Anina, I am certain he still misses you! He always refuses to let me read your letters out to him – but he secretly looks at them when I leave the room.'

Anna told her sister about their friend, Gerard Belringer, who was 'an important adviser' to the Chancellor of the Exchequer. Liese said, 'They will all be so impressed when I tell them at home! And I shall tell Father all about your beautiful home! And your clever, handsome children, and how well Otto looks after you!'

'Yes – and make sure Hermann knows it too, please!'

'Ah yes. Hermann. How our boys hero-worship the Famous General! He has been awarded the Iron Cross, you know. After France. Even Margarethe thinks he's wonderful.' Anna looked sharply at her sister. Liese said quietly, 'We've never told her.' She took Anna's hands and looked at her seriously. 'She is a very happy young lady, Anina. I never even think about it myself now – except sometimes when she suddenly exclaims about something and for a moment I think – it's Anna! But she is a daughter we can all be proud of.'

*

Liverpool and Manchester – 1905

The following spring, Otto and Anna moved to a detached house in Everton Road where they had much more space and Otto had room for a grand piano, which he could now afford. He was still working for Liverpool Council as a piano tuner and as a part-time piano teacher at the school, but most of his income came from giving private lessons to more serious music students. Germans and music sat well together in people's minds, and his pupils liked to boast about their 'German professor'. Otto wrote postcards to Edgar in Devon, *'We are going up in the world! I think it is all thanks to Herr Beethoven!'*

52

There was a small garden with some fruit trees and a greenhouse against one wall of their new home which saw almost as much of Otto as his music room. He would wander out there as soon as he had taken breakfast and would spend hours sowing seeds and gazing at his neat rows of trays, sighing with pleasure. His strings of climbing tomato plants, his seedling violets and his pots of begonias and geraniums all moved him to sing gentle arias under his breath. Sometimes Anna saw him clearly conducting his plants in a great ode to joy.

Wilhelm and Leah had moved to Manchester, where Wilhelm had begun work as a salesman for a newly established northern publishing company, the idea of a wealthy Liverpool banker, Sir Ronald Golding, who had already made his fortune investing in specifically northern businesses, particularly in shipping and cotton.

He also liked to support smaller enterprises, and had recently bought a failing weekly magazine with offices in Manchester. He had seen that there could be a market for popular family fiction written around the lives of men and women living and working in the north of England, in the countryside and in the cities, in the farms and the mills, the mines, factories and dockyards. He had many friends who were journalists on Liverpool and Manchester newspapers and they were soon turning out short, easy-to-read novels in their spare time. It had been a shrewd investment. Written by journalists, although classified as romantic fiction, the stories had an authentic feel to them and quickly began to reach a growing market. Other local authors and even well-established London authors began to submit books and short stories on the same themes.

For Wilhelm, this career move proved a great success. Given his rather diffident nature, he had once not seemed cut out to be a salesman, but his marriage to the strong-minded Leah had given him new confidence. He had always been an avid reader, and now his enthusiasm for these romanticised fictions about the life and times of people whose experiences he knew so well was something he could convey very effectively to the bookshop managers on his list.

His new job meant Wilhelm now had to be away from home, sometimes for long periods, so he bought a dog to guard Leah and the children when he was away – a big bullmastiff they called Tess. Tess looked fierce, but was in fact so timid and gentle that Leah doubted she would really do much in the way of protecting them, but they both agreed that one look at her would be enough to scare away any intruder. He and Leah now had three sons, Albert, Edgar and little Leo, and there was another baby on the way. Since the move to Manchester they had had to give up singing with the Mossley Hill choral singers, but they both enjoyed supporting their local church choir.

Otto's sister Clara had trained to become a nursery school teacher, and her brothers, Otto and Edgar, had bought her a lease on her own little flat in Liverpool. Clara had always been like a second mother to Otto's children, especially Wilhelm, and during the school holidays she would spend as much time as she could in Manchester helping Leah with her growing family.

*

In the General Election of January 1906, the Liberals, with H. H. Asquith as Chancellor of the Exchequer, won a landslide victory. The Conservatives lost more than half their seats, including that of their leader, Arthur Balfour, in Manchester East. A newly formed Labour Party, with Keir Hardie as leader, won 29 seats.

Everton Road, Liverpool – 1906
A few days after Easter 1906, Gerard Belringer and Alice Lohmann were married.

My dear Boy!

The Good is let loose in the World, Lad! And it is coming to you today! For it is your Birthday! And we all join to give it speed towards you.

I hope that these lines will find you in the best of health, happiness and prosperity!

And may the good come in tumbling amongst <u>all</u> the Members of your Domestic Empire.

We have heard <u>Nothing</u> from you, for such a long – long – long time. There is an old proverb, and it says: no news is good news. However, I am such a procrastinating correspondent myself that I have no room for grumbling.

I am to announce that Alice will be married this month (at long, long last!) to Gerard Belringer next Wednesday at the Register Office. I thought the day would never arrive! Lunch will be served at our 'new!' house which you have yet to see. The young couple will leave here late in the afternoon for their new home. They had intended to go abroad for a fortnight, but Gerard has to go down to London on some political business – Again! – and he now says that Alice would like it better in the warmer season. Well, you must think what you will of that.

Now if you and Leah and the children, or you alone, could come over? You shall find a warm welcome. Papa is not so well as he might be. But we are jogging on.

How is your youngest baby? Name unknown!

Now I will close.

Love and Greetings to All!!!

And take my best love for yourself.

Mother

Letter from Anna to Wilhelm 1 April 1906

5

Humbug

11 September 1908

'You English are mad, mad, mad as March hares. What has come over you that you are so completely given over to suspicions quite unworthy of a great nation? What more can I do than I have done? I declared with all the emphasis at my command, in my speech at Guildhall, that my heart is set upon peace, and that it is one of my dearest wishes to live on the best of terms with England. Have I ever been false to my word? Falsehood and prevarication are alien to my nature. My actions ought to speak for themselves, but you listen not to them but to those who misinterpret and distort them. That is a personal insult which I feel and resent. To be forever misjudged, to have my repeated offers of friendship weighed and scrutinized with jealous, mistrustful eyes, taxes my patience severely. I have said time after time that I am a friend of England, and your press -- at least, a considerable section of it -- but the people of England refuse my proffered hand and insinuates that the other holds a dagger.'

Interview in the *Daily Telegraph* with Kaiser Wilhelm

Liverpool – 15 August 1908

A growing feeling of prejudice against Germans was becoming palpable. Germany's industrial and military growth had been explosive, and new Germany watchers were growing increasingly anxious about the Kaiser's territorial ambitions. The press had quickly picked up on an atmosphere of political nervousness, and cartoons appeared daily, always depicting Germans as gross and greedy in the representative figure of Kaiser Wilhelm. Anna found herself growing more and more depressed whenever Otto read anything out to her from the newspapers.

One morning one of her closest friends, Muriel Cartwright, dropped in to see Anna, and repeated some rude comment she had read about the Kaiser. On seeing the surprised expression on Anna's face, Muriel had laughed and said, 'Of course, my dear, we never think of you and Otto as being in the least bit like *those* Germans.'

Shortly after Muriel had left, a letter arrived from Liese saying that '*Mr Belringer*' had recently called on them unexpectedly and had introduced himself as '*your niece, Alice's, new husband.*' They had all been charmed by him, and he had asked them to introduce him to the Baron and Hermann – which they had been delighted to do of course....

Anna gave a sigh, and found herself assailed with a wave of homesickness. A sudden burst of noise in the street outside made Anna put down the letter, stand up stiffly and go to the window. It was just a group of children playing some wild game in the road.

Anna thought gloomily, 'Our children are all grown. I am over fifty years old and we have lived in Liverpool for more than thirty years.'

Everything that had happened to her before they came here seemed like a story about somebody else. She had buried her memories for so long. But now she found she wanted to remember why she had left so much behind.

*

Boyenstrasse, Berlin Stadt – May 1872

'Anna?'

Hearing her father's voice, Anna came out of the salon to greet him in the hall. With him was a tall, fair-haired young man in the uniform of a cavalry officer. Her father, Emil, beamed at her.

'There you are, Anna! Look who I have found at our front door! Herr Oberstleutnant Hermann von Treitschke! He has returned to us at last – and he comes from France – a conquering hero.'

Hermann clicked his heels together and taking hold of one of Anna's hands kissed it, smiling up at her as though they shared a secret. She recognised that knowing smile. Until his family had left Berlin for Heidelberg eight years earlier, Hermann had been a school friend of one of her elder brothers, and whenever he came to their house he always teased her. She had once looked out of the window and seen him throwing stones at a cat in the street running alongside the canal. She had run down the stairs through the hall, seized one of her father's display sabres from the wall and with it raised threateningly over her head had flown out of the house towards Hermann, who had raced off down the street laughing, raising his own hands in mock alarm. She was very glad when he and his family had left Berlin.

She wiped some leaves off her hands where she had been arranging flowers in the other room, and looked at the quiet, handsome gentleman, in the uniform of a cavalry officer, but who still had a way of looking at her with gleam in his blue eyes that unsettled her. From the saloon behind them came the sound of someone talking in a low voice, and a piano being tuned.

'How tall you have grown, Donna Anna.'

She looked down, pulling a wry face, and Hermann turned to Emil, 'I think that perhaps Donna Anna does not have a very favourable memory of me, Sir. The last time we met, Anna chased me down the road with a great sword. I was very afraid of her!'

Anna looked up sharply, 'You were throwing stones at a little cat!' She paused for a moment, suddenly tearful at the memory. 'You hurt it.'

Hermann said in surprise, 'But Anina! It was just a stray cat!'

Emil said, 'Those cats are all a confounded nuisance. I would drown the lot of them if they didn't keep down the rats. Now, Anna, I have arranged with Hermann that, while he is stationed in Berlin, he and one of his fellow officers and their man must stay here, in the rooms at the top of the house. It's time we started to use our upstairs apartments for the purpose they were built. Hermann is going to bring Herr Oberstleutnant Ziegler to view the rooms next week.'

'I am very grateful, Sir. It will be very good to be lodging with friends.'

'Your father is resident in Berlin permanently now, I understand?'

'Yes – all the family have returned from Heidelberg. He and my mother both asked me to present their compliments to you, Sir, and hope there can soon be a reunion of old friends.' Hermann clicked his heels together again and bowed first to

Emil and then to Anna. 'And, of course, they send their compliments to your daughter. Anina, your father has kindly given me permission to call on you. I do hope I may have the honour of accompanying you to the Leipzig Music Festival next week?'

From the salon had come the sound of one note being played repeatedly by the Klavierstimmer.

*

Staring out of the window, Anna found herself trembling uncontrollably. She waited until she felt calmer and then went out into the garden to find Otto where she knew he would be – in his greenhouse.

'What humbugs the English are!' she announced. Humbugs had become Anna's favourite word since Wilhelm had given her *Little Dorrit* for her birthday. Otto looked up from his potting and smiled at her. 'Who is being a humbug today, Anna?'

'All of them! Muriel Cartwright.'

'Oh dear. What has Muriel said now? She can be rather.... But you know what she's like – she doesn't really mean ...'

'It's not just Muriel. All the English – humbugs.... I think it is time we ... went.'

'Went? Went where? We belong here now, Anna. And you know, not all the English are humbugs. Are our kind neighbours, who have all helped us so very much since we came, humbugs? They are even teaching me many of the secrets of gardening – it is like learning a new kind of music. Are our grandchildren humbugs? You mustn't worry about some silly thing Muriel has said. Come now, Anina!'

'I thought that our idea about being 'free citizens of the world' meant we would travel about the world ... even return to Germany if we wanted to ... surely it might be better now ... Gerard frequently goes there – my sister writes that he called on them recently ... I didn't think we meant to stay away forever.'

'This is all because of what the newspapers are saying, isn't it? You know how they love to spread alarm and dismay. At the moment it is all the fault of the wretched Kaiser....' Otto put his hand up to touch his eyes.

'I am sorry, Otto. I don't mean to give you one of your headaches. I feel better now I've talked to you.' She kissed him, and walked back into the house. He smiled and turned back to his tomatoes.

As it was a fine summer's afternoon and Otto had no pupils to see, after lunch they decided to go out for a walk down to the estuary. They stood for a few moments in Salthouse Dock watching a group of men at work hauling in and coiling ropes along the wharf, dwarf masters of a giant ship with flapping rigging that wallowed heavily at bay in the scummy water.

As they wandered along the quays, the business and the steady rhythm of river life, the smell of the fish and the cries of the circling sea-gulls over their heads steadied and stimulated them both. Crowded Mersey ferries were busily criss-crossing backwards and forwards, and plumes of smoke rose from the factories straight up into the windless sky and they counted forty ships moored alongside the warehouses that stretched down the length of the river; they stood and watched in silence as a vast liner was led out of Queen's dock towards the estuary by ridiculously small tugs.

Anna imagined walking across to the ticket office, buying their tickets, boarding some great red-funnelled steamship or a huge, stately liner. She could see them leaning over the rails, waving goodbye to all their friends and family as they slipped out of port on their way to ... well, anywhere they wanted ... citizens of the world.... She began to say, 'Don't you ever think ...?' but as Otto looked at her enquiringly, she sighed, and shook her head. 'Nothing – it's all just humbug. Let's go home.'

'You do love that word, Anna!'

'It is a very good word for the English, Otto.'

'The English are perhaps of all humanity the greatest "humbugs". They love more than anything in the World pretence; and the farther away the reality is from this sham they create out of their imagination, the more dearly they love the sham'.

Anna's diary, 15 August 1908

6

Hans

Liverpool – June 1914

'How Hans has grown! A giant! I would not have recognised him but for the blonde hair and beautiful manners! We are all charmed and so happy he has come to see his 'English' cousins!'

Letter from Anna to Liese 16 June

In the middle of June, Hans Schindler, Anna's young nephew, came to stay. They had met him only once before, in 1904 when he was a little boy and his mother, Liese, had brought him with her on a short visit. Since then Hans had grown to over six foot and was now a shy, handsome young man of twenty. Frederick at twenty-five and Emily at twenty-three were both still living at home with their parents. Emily was studying at teacher training college and Frederick was working in a chemist's shop as apprentice to the pharmacist.

'Oh! Oh look!' When Frederick appeared downstairs to greet his cousin for the first time, Otto and Anna had both laughed at the sight of their son, like a black haired, brown-eyed elf, shaking hands with a blond, blue-eyed giant.

Hans was studying architecture in Leipzig, and planned to spend the summer in England camping in the Lake District, sketching and painting landscapes, with Anna and Otto's home as his base. Otto was tolerant as they chattered away in German, although from time to time he would say quietly, 'Now, Anna, you must let Hans speak English or he will never improve. It is what he has come for, after all, not just to paint.'

From the moment he arrived, Anna loved her enormous, smiling nephew.

'Grandfather is going to be 90 years old next year – and is still ordering our father about! He is unbelievable.' Anna was sorting through a pile of Otto's music while Hans was giving her the family news. She looked up, surprised.

'But Papa is not still working, surely?'

'He goes in each morning to keep them all … "up to the mark"!'

'Oh my Papa! At 90! He will never change! My poor sister! And your poor father! And young Nicolai – he is pursuing his career in the army?'

'Yes. Nicko is now Oberstleutnant.'

'Dear me! But I hope you are not also thinking of going into the army, Hans?'

'No. Generaloberst von Treitschke was very keen that I should – but I am not like Nicko or Leon – who is also serving now. I will have to do my National Service too, of course. As soon as I get home I think.'

'I don't think they will be able to find any boots big enough for your feet! So perhaps they will let you off! Artists and architects are meant for creating beautiful places, not for knocking them down.' Anna straightened up from sorting out the sheet music, and smiled at him.

'And your big sister ... Margarethe?'

'Oh she is such a bossy one! Just like grandfather. And Nicko *is* building something. He is building a bridge in Bosnia Herzegovina.'

'A bridge?'

'Yes. I believe that is so.'

Anna smiled. 'Well, that is good. But little Margarethe – she has a sweetheart?'

'Yes. She has a serious young man. He is a soldier also, in Uncle Hermann's regiment.'

Emily had been staying with a friend from College the day that Hans arrived, and when she came home she and Freddie took their cousin to see the sights of Liverpool. Anna called to Otto to come quickly to look at them through the window as they set off down the road together – Emily marching briskly in the lead, head in the air, swinging her umbrella, Freddie behind her chattering nineteen to the dozen and gesticulating wildly to Hans, who was bending gracefully over his cousin's bobbing head, like a tall ship being towed out to sea by two bustling tug boats.

The three cousins took the tramcar down to the pier head and after looking round the city centre, they took the ferry across the Mersey to Birkenhead. With his great height and almost white blonde hair, Hans was receiving friendly smiles and teasing remarks called out to him wherever he went. After lunch Emily showed him round her college. She introduced Hans to her tutor, Mr Carter, and apologised for not attending his class that morning but Hans was her cousin, newly arrived from Germany, and she was showing him round Liverpool. Mr Carter was very friendly and as they were leaving he said teasingly to Hans, 'Miss Logan had given me the impression that her cousin was a young boy of ten that it would be her duty to look after when he came to stay. I see that it is not being such an onerous duty after all!'

After leaving Mr Carter, they joined Freddie in the canteen for coffee and were just sitting down at a table when an elegantly dressed girl came over to greet Emily. Freddie and Hans both stood up.

'Hello, Emily.'

'Oh. Hello, Mary.'

Mary stood looking at Emily expectantly.

'Oh. I see. Yes. Sorry. Mary, may I introduce ... I think you know my brother, Freddie? And this is Hans Schindler, a friend from Germany,' said Emily. 'Hans, Freddie – this is Miss Underwood. Mary is studying music here at the College.'

Freddie smiled and shook the hand Mary offered. 'Hello, Mary.' Mary smiled, but her gaze quickly turned to Hans who bowed his head and clicked his heels formally.

'Which part of Germany are you from, Mr Schindler?'

'Our family home is in Berlin, but now I am actually studying architecture in Leipzig, Miss Underwood.'

'What do you think of Liverpool? I hope you are impressed! We are all very proud of our city.'

'The architecture is indeed very beautiful. And Liverpool people are all so very friendly.'

'So I should hope! Oh, please do sit down, Hans and Freddie. I'm only sorry I must dash away now. I hope we meet again.'

'Hans, young men in England don't click their heels,' Emily said when she had gone.

'Actually, Emily, in Germany also it is not so often these days. But I thought I was expected to put on a 'German' show for your friend.' Hans turned to Freddie, 'Why did Emily say to that young lady that I am a friend, and not your cousin?'

Emily said quickly, 'I'm sorry Hans. It's just.... I don't want everyone asking me a lot of tiresome questions about our family background.'

'Questions? About us? Or about Germany? Is that so difficult? Surely your father is known as a professor is he not? Your tutor seemed happy to have a student with a German cousin .... Even this tram we have just been riding on – was a fine German tram.'

'Yes. But ... Freddie and I are not German. We feel English. We do things the English way. Very few people at College know that our parents are German.'

Freddie seemed to come out of a reverie and said suddenly, 'I don't mind – I tell everybody. But we don't know why our parents left Germany in the first place. Except for some idea of our father's that we are now Citizens of the World. Do you know why they left, Hans?'

'Well, only that – my mother says it was for the best. It was after we had come to stay with you before, she told me that your mother had had to make a difficult choice to leave Germany – but that your father is a very good man. And it was the right thing. That is all she said.'

'Tell us about Berlin.'

'Berlin is a little like Liverpool in one way, because everybody knows by your accent if you come from Berlin. I seem to remember you all teaching me to say English words with a funny accent when I was here before.'

'Say something with a Berlin accent.'

'*Ist heut festlicher Tag; da putzt sich jeder so schon er mag.* But your mother is *ein Berliner*! So she has also this accent.'

'Mother! With an accent! Never!'

'Oh it is very good, the Berlin accent. Very posh. Is that the right word? Our great grandmother's side of the family were Huguenots – who like so many thousands came to Berlin as refugees, and so the Berlin dialect has a little French lilt to it. So perhaps it is OK?'

'I never knew we were descended from Huguenots! I always thought we were Prussians, and I think we are also partly Jewish. On our father's side. I thought that might have been part of the reason ...'

'So? You have Jewish, Huguenot and Prussian blood – but Emily wishes only to be English!'

When they returned in the evening Emily went straight upstairs to her room, and the two young men went into the kitchen to talk to Anna as she prepared the evening meal.

'What did you think of Liverpool, Hans?'

'It is very beautiful. There are so many fine buildings, and we crossed the river on a wonderful small ferry and talked to many people. Everyone is so very friendly here. People smile at you or make a joke. Much more than in Berlin. We are all more serious I think.'

'It was really only the girls who were smiling at Hans, Mother. You should have seen them! Every girl we saw – on the ferry and in the park and at Emily's college. Everywhere.'

The following Saturday Freddie took Hans to call on Otto's sister, Clara Lohmann, in her little flat. Clara, like everyone else, exclaimed at the size of him and gave them both an enormous tea. The following Monday, Hans took the train to Manchester on his own to visit Will and Leah and their children, Albert, Edgar, Leo, Philip, Molly (the only girl) Clifford and the baby, six month old Sam. He was welcomed enthusiastically and afterwards he told Anna and Otto that he had felt like Gulliver in Lilliput. When he fell asleep in the garden after lunch, the boys had removed his shoes and socks and undone his shirt without his noticing.

'I woke up to find myself almost naked!'

'Whatever did Leah say?'

'Oh Leah was very, very angry. They were all sent to their rooms. She did not think it funny at all. She is a very stern mother I think.'

'Very strict,' Otto agreed. 'Even with poor old Will. She was very unfortunate in finding the only lazy German in England to marry!'

'Wilhelm is not lazy!' said Anna indignantly. 'He has always worked very hard. He is an intellectual. And perhaps he is a dreamer, sometimes. That is all.'

That night Hans accompanied Otto to a concert, where almost as soon as the music began, he fell into a deep, peaceful slumber. Otto woke him in the interval and Hans said apologetically, 'I love music, Uncle, but before I know what is happening, I always seem to drift off to sleep.'

'So what do you think of your big cousin?' Anna asked her daughter while Hans and Otto were out.

'Are all German men like that?'

'Like Hans? I wish I could say so. I don't remember anyone so tall and handsome … or so gentle when I was a girl … or perhaps I wouldn't have looked twice at your father!'

'I mean, are German boys all so formal and polite? Hans is a bit – is pompous the right word?'

'Sometimes it is difficult for sensitive young men to know how to behave when they are with a beautiful woman!'

Emily scowled. 'Don't be silly, Mother.' Anna smiled to herself and raised her eyes to heaven.

A week later Hans was preparing to set off for the Lake District to begin his painting tour. He planned to come home every week or ten days to bath and restock his camping and painting equipment. 'But if the weather is perfect – I may not be able to tear myself from the mountains!'

Emily said, 'But Hans mustn't go before your dinner on Friday, Papa!'

'Oh yes, Hans, you must stay for that,' said Anna.

There was to be a big formal dinner on the last Friday of June, in the Adelphi Hotel, in Otto's honour. One of his students, Edward Golding, had just won a place at the prestigious Royal College of Music in London. Edward was the son of Sir Ronald Golding, the owner of the publishing company that Wilhelm now worked for. Sir Ronald had been disappointed when his son had not done well at school at first, but now Edward was a son to be proud of, and to show his gratitude he was holding this dinner which was to be as much in Otto's honour as to congratulate his son.

Hans said, 'I will certainly wish to stay for a dinner in honour of Uncle Otto.'

'Edward has worked hard for his great success,' Otto said firmly. And that is what we shall celebrate. All I gave him was a little self-confidence to believe he could do it.'

'Is that what it takes to become a successful musician, Uncle Otto? Self-confidence?'

'Of course not!' Anna exclaimed. Otto smiled wryly. 'Or all Otto's pupils would be at the Royal College, because he always gives them confidence in themselves. But they are not all such good musicians. They do all receive one important thing – a love and understanding of music which will last a lifetime. That is the really wonderful thing he does.'

'That is a great tribute I think, Uncle Otto.'

Otto smiled and shook his head at his wife.

Anna went on, 'It is all in Otto's honour, pay no attention to what he says, and as members of his family we are all invited.'

Hans said, 'And it is to be a formal occasion? I must wear my evening dress?'

'Yes, certainly. You will look wonderful.'

'But I am learning that some English people do not like us Germans very much at the moment? Emily doesn't like anyone to know it.'

'Oh – well, the Kaiser says things that people here don't like and then they think that if you are German you probably think the same way as him. But we think he is mad.'

'In Germany too, he says things that annoy people. But he is related to the English Royal family is he not?'

'Yes indeed. But people here don't like that either.'

After supper that evening, they all sat in the music room and Anna played the piano. Emily sat curled up on the window sill, half reading a book, half gazing out into the garden. Hans sat opposite her, sketching. She glanced over to him and saw he was looking at her intently. He was looking down at his sketch pad and then back at her face, his hand moving over the page. Emily felt a powerful tingling sensation across her scalp and down her neck. She was surprised by how entirely pleasurable the feeling was and how much she hoped he wouldn't stop.

'What are you drawing?'

'I am drawing a hedgehog, Miss Emily.'

'A hedgehog! Why a hedgehog?'

'Because hedgehogs are charming but if you approach them they roll up into a tight prickly ball.'

Emily returned to her book.

*

Liverpool – June 25

'What time is your photographer coming, Otto?'

'At about ten. He said he would need time to arrange his things, and decide the best place to position us.'

'Us? Oh no, Otto!'

'I have told them that no picture of me would be permitted that did not include you, my dear. So it is agreed. They will photograph both of us together.'

'But Otto! Of course Sir Ronald doesn't want a picture of a tired old woman – he wants to see the great creator of prodigies!'

'Well I wish him to see this old man and his old woman.'

'But no, Otto! What would I wear? I don't want to spoil my new dress for the occasion.'

Otto thought for a moment. 'I think we should wear our travelling clothes, like people who just happen to be resting for a moment in the middle of their long journey through life.'

When the photographer from the *Liverpool News* arrived, he immediately began setting up his apparatus around the piano in the music room. Otto came in to say, 'Mr Sims, I wonder … would you mind taking our portrait outside in the garden instead of in here? It is such a beautiful day and we would so like to be photographed wearing our travelling clothes.'

Mr Sims dismantled his ladders and lighting stands and followed Otto out through the back door onto the terrace. It was a very warm day, with a gentle wind blowing. Mr Sims and Otto persuaded Anna to sit demurely on a wicker garden chair in the lee of the house, with Otto standing beside her.

The photographer went in and out of the house, collecting some of Anna's potted plants to display artistically around them. Then he disappeared for several minutes under the black cloth draped over his camera. Finally he emerged and said to Anna, 'Madam, do you by any chance own such a thing as a fur stole or some such garment?'

'Yes! But it is very old. I hardly ever wear it, but as it happens I have recently taken it out of mothballs in preparation for the dinner being held in my husband's honour.'

Mr Sims' eyes lit up. 'Indeed. I shall be at the event myself, taking photographs on behalf of the newspaper. I believe it is to be a celebration in honour of Sir Ronald's son?'

'The celebration is in honour of my husband, for helping young Edward to get into the Royal College, and for all the good work that he has done teaching the love of music to the young people of this city.' Anna said firmly.

'Anna!'

Mr Sims bowed respectfully. 'As I know it is for such an auspicious occasion, perhaps you would allow me to add a certain richness to the setting in which I take your photograph, with the addition of your fur wrap?'

'But I never wear a fur wrap when I'm travelling!' Anna went inside shaking her head and called to Emily to find it for her. Mr Sims asked Otto if there was such a thing as a broom he could use. Otto went to his garden shed and returned with one, and Mr Sims began sweeping the ground in front of Anna's chair. Emily came down with the wrap, full of curiosity, but when Anna reluctantly started to put it on, Mr Sims said, 'Oh, no, no, Madam. This is my idea....' He laid the long stole reverently down on the ground he had just swept. Otto and Anna both peered down at it, and then looked at Emily, and all three of them burst out laughing.

Later that day, Gerard and Alice came over to meet Hans, and they brought with them their daughter, five-year-old Maisie. The little girl was thrilled by Hans, who galloped round the garden with her riding on his back shrieking with laughter.

'Now, Miranda Violet – that is quite enough now,' said her father sternly. 'I need to talk to Hans and Grandfather. I want you to go and help your Grandmamma indoors.'

'No. I love Hans. He is my giant horse.'

'Come on, Maisie,' said Emily brightly. 'Come with me and I'll show you my best dolly.'

'Have you got a dolly?' asked Maisie in wonder. 'My mummy says she's too old to have a dolly.'

'Oh I hope I shall never grow too old for Dolly,' said Emily. Alice was in the kitchen talking to her mother and helping to get the food ready.

The three men stood together in the garden and Gerard said, 'I think it might be wise for Hans to return home to Germany as soon as possible.'

'But I have only just arrived!' exclaimed Hans. 'Why ever should I leave so soon?'

'I hope it's nothing ... but I am afraid it looks as though Germany is expecting trouble from the East.'

'Oh, I know all about that,' said Hans airily. 'My brother tells me we are quite prepared for any trouble that may come from there. And it is Austria-Hungary, not Germany, who will have to deal with it. Our soldiers are only there helping to build a bridge.'

Otto looked at Gerard who was not saying anything but looking up at the sky as though for inspiration. Finally he said, 'I sincerely hope it will all come to nothing. But if matters begin taking a turn for the worse, I am afraid that Hans must make a swift return home. Shall we go back in? My little girl will be demanding more of your attention, Hans, I fear.'

He linked arms with Otto as they walked back towards the house. 'Otto, you must tell me all about this great event tomorrow night. I am unfortunately unable to attend. I have some very pressing business to attend to in London tomorrow, but Alice will come. I hear it is all being held in your honour.'

'The family are all very excited about it, of course. But it is really for young Edward – not for me.'

'Sir Ronald is a good friend, and I happen to know that it is his idea to honour you for all you have done, not just for his family, but for the city.'

Otto smiled. 'Yes, I see. Nothing to do with you of course, Gerard.'

*

On the night of the dinner Otto and the family, including Hans, Wilhelm and Leah, stood to have their photograph taken by Mr Sims, this time outside St George's Hall. The story behind the event had already been reported in the newspaper that day, and there were two or three other reporters waiting for guests to arrive, and another group of about a dozen people were standing outside the hall with placards that read 'No Huns Wanted Here!' They began to shout as soon as they realised Otto and his family had arrived, shaking their placards at Otto and Hans particularly.

Sir Ronald hurried outside with several of his other guests, including his son, Edward, and publicly welcomed Otto and his family before quickly ushering them into the hall, where there was applause as they entered. Anna had been in tears, but she was soon calmed by the elegance of their surroundings – the huge room lit by dozens of candelabras and the long tables of beautifully dressed guests being served by uniformed waiters – and the speeches in praise of Otto. She was able to write to her sister the next morning with news of what a wonderful, marvellous occasion it had been, and how everyone had admired not just Otto but also their beautiful giant of a nephew!

Early on Saturday morning, Hans left for the Lake District. Anna and Emily stood outside and waved him goodbye as he set out for the station riding the bicycle Freddie had lent him, loaded up with his painting and camping equipment. Over the next few days he would be living on his own, camping on a hill looking over Lake Windermere. He missed seeing the headlines in the next week's *Evening News* declaring that on Sunday 28 June, Archduke Hans Ferdinand (heir to the Austro-Hungarian throne) and his wife, Sofia, the Duchess of Hohenberg, had been assassinated while on an official visit to Sarajevo.

7

Heat Wave

Liverpool – 6 July 1914

The news of the assassination in Sarajevo left the civic calm of Liverpool unshaken. Most people, especially the young, had been enjoying the unusually warm summer weather all June and now July had begun and was bringing even more sunshine to the city. People were shocked and felt some sympathy for the young Archduke and his Duchess, but this heat wave meant that few people were taking life too seriously.

Otto, however, was reading the newspaper reports with increasing anxiety as Anna prepared their breakfast each morning.

'The murder of the Archduke and his wife was the outcome of a Servian conspiracy.... But that this will be credited throughout Austria and Hungary is somewhat doubtful, and an outburst of anti-Servian feeling there must be looked for.... That is what is to be feared just now – a weak acquiescence in racial enmity. The comments in Berlin on Austria's activities in the Balkans indicate that Germany feels directly interested in what is happening.'

Liverpool Echo, 6 July

Next morning Otto looked up from his paper, 'Well let's hope that this at least is a good sign, Anna – listen:

"The Kaiser has left Berlin for a summer cruise off the coast of Norway on board his yacht Hohenzollern."'

Anna laughed, 'You see, Otto! I told you the Kaiser could have no intention of going to war! You worry too much.'

They were still finishing their breakfast when Gerard Belringer let himself in and called from the front hall, 'Otto? Where is Hans?'

Otto got up and went into the hall to join him.

'Good morning, Gerard. We're in the kitchen. Can we offer you some coffee? Hans is in the Lake District.'

'When are you expecting him back?'

'He left last week – the day before the news broke, so he won't know anything about it. He said he would be back in about ten days for a change of clothes.'

'Tell him I must talk to him as soon as he returns. It is vitally important.'

'But … then, do you want me to contact him to bring him back sooner?'

'Is that possible?'

'I could send a telegram to the farmer where we arranged for him to go in an emergency and where we can leave messages for him. He would get it, but not necessarily today or tomorrow. I don't think the farmer would be willing to go out and search for him. He could be anywhere.'

'Well – no, never mind. But as soon as he reappears – I want to be the first to know. The problem is I shall have to go away soon myself. Does he have any papers with him?'

'I'm not sure. I don't think so.'

'No. Right. Well when he returns, just make sure he stays here until I get back, will you? Don't let him leave again.'

'It is because of all this Balkan business I imagine, Gerard?'

'Yes. No. Everyone is trying hard to calm things down, but that blasted Kaiser is quite determined to seize this opportunity and make the most of it.'

'But I was reading to Anna that the Kaiser has gone away on holiday....'

'Yes, he has – the devious old so-and-so. But we all know he's not going to let this chance go by if he can help it. He isn't fooling anyone. Now, Otto, you must please tell Hans as soon as he returns that he must be ready to return home at once.'

Otto walked Gerard to the gate, where a uniformed driver was waiting in a motor car, the man looking straight ahead pretending to ignore an excited crowd of boys that had gathered round. 'Do you like going about in that thing?' Otto asked as he watched Gerard getting in beside the driver.

'Sorry to be in such a rush, Otto. But … well … you understand. I'm sorry – I must go.' He put on a pair of goggles and told the driver to move off.

'Give Alice our love,' Otto called, and waved as the car moved slowly off down the sunny street. One of the bolder boys charged forward and leapt up onto the running board beside the chauffeur and hung on for a few yards, and then jumped off again before they turned the corner. He ran back to his friends waving his cap triumphantly. Otto went back into the house. Anna looked at him expectantly, but he was lost in thought. 'Gerard has a new car,' he said absently.

Hans reappeared from the Lake District three days after Gerard Belringer's visit, looking tanned and fit. He had come home with the bicycle and some watercolour sketches he had made, but had left most of his painting equipment at the farm. Otto went with him to see Belringer, but when they got there Alice told them, 'Gerard's abroad somewhere. He said he didn't expect to be away for long. I'll tell him you want to see him as soon as he gets home.'

'Well it is more a case of him wanting to see Hans. Tell him that Hans is home and that he won't be going back to the Lakes without talking to him.'

'Poor Hans! What a funny holiday you are having!'

That evening Anna prepared a special 'German' dinner in Hans's honour. Wilhelm – or Will, as Leah now insisted that they all call him – joined them. Anna had written out a menu for the dinner and placed it on the dining room table in a silver frame that was usually only on display at Christmas.

When the family were all seated, Hans read the menu card written in Anna's immaculate Gothic script:

Fladlesuppe

Gekochter Schinken mit Salat und die Kartoffel

Brathering

Apfel im Schlafrock

'*Fladlesuppe*,' Hans said out loud, 'for all us Citizens of the World! Now this, Will, really is an authentic German dinner. This would be exactly the menu for a special occasion in my mother's house.'

Anna smiled as she ladled out the soup into bowls from a big tureen, mounted on an iron stand in front of her on the table.

Emily said, 'How did you get on in the Lake District, Hans?'

'I must show you what I have done. I am quite pleased. The sun shone every day so the light was magnificent, especially in the late afternoons. I hope I have caught something of the majesty and wildness of your mountains.'

'Whereabouts in the Lakes were you?'

'I was at Lake Windermere – do you know it?

'Oh yes – that's where Wordsworth lived. I have always wanted to see it. Why don't we all go there? Do let's. We could have a holiday in the Lakes and see what Hans is painting.'

Hans said, 'That would be an honour for me!' As they were dipping their bread into the bowls of soup, Hans turned to Wilhelm, 'And when you come to Germany, Will, I will show you Dresden. This is the most beautiful baroque city in all Europe. In the whole world I think. And we might even go across into Austria to Salzburg ...'

When Hans had first arrived in Liverpool they had all talked about the possibility of Wilhelm going back to Berlin with him for a short visit when it was time for him to return to Germany. Clara had already been asked and agreed to go over to stay in Manchester to help Leah with the children, and Alice had said that she and Maisie would go over for a few days too, as Maisie loved playing with her big cousins.

Otto, who had seemed wrapped up in his own thoughts, now looked up sharply. 'I am sorry. There is no question of Wilhelm – Will – being able to come back with you, Hans, and especially not to Austria. They won't be welcoming foreigners there at the moment.'

Hans looked astonished.

William said, 'Hans won't have heard the news.'

'What news is this?' asked Hans.

Emily said, 'Oh Hans! Don't you know? Some Servians have assassinated the Austrian Archduke by throwing a bomb into his carriage, and when it failed to explode, they shot him. And his wife. Poor things.'

'No! But this is terrible. When was this?'

'It must have been the day you left us. Father thinks it means you have to return to Germany immediately. We're waiting for Gerard Belringer to come back from his business trip somewhere to advise us. Until he does, he asks that you stay here with us.'

Hans looked at his aunt and uncle for confirmation, and Otto nodded gravely.

Hans said, 'I'm so sorry to have missed all the excitement. I never look at newspapers when I am in the hills. But – how sad – have they caught the perpetrators? What is happening now?'

'Who knows? They don't know who was behind the assassination, let alone arrested anybody.'

'I had better read my letters from home after dinner. Perhaps in Germany they already know more.'

For the rest of the dinner they discussed the differences between Germany and England. Anna exclaimed at the awfulness of English cooking and how glad she was that at least in Liverpool there were plenty of German butchers, bakers and pastry makers so they could eat properly at home.

'As you will be staying with us until Gerard returns, Hans, you may see what I am talking about. Emily and her boyfriend both eat simply dreadful food.'

'Mother!'

'Of course, I shall very much enjoy staying here, Aunt Anna. But I shall need to return to Windermere to collect my painting things. I want to turn my sketches of Emily and Alice into proper portraits while I am here, if they will permit it, so I can show everyone at home what beautiful cousins we have.'

After dinner, Hans went upstairs to the bedroom he shared with Freddie, who had remained silent all through the meal and when he had finished had quietly gone up to his room. He was lying on his bed with a book on his chest, staring at the ceiling. He glanced at Hans who smiled at him and sat down on his own bed to read his letters.

Downstairs, Anna and Emily cleared away the supper things in the kitchen. Wilhelm and his father went through to the front parlour. A noisy gang of children were playing in the street outside, and their voices shouting out the rules of their game to each other made conversation difficult. Wilhelm got up and closed the windows. As he came back to sit down again he said,

'Why don't you ever want to go back to Germany yourself, Father?'

Otto smiled, 'Because I am very happy here.'

'Yes, but Germany is still your homeland surely?'

'Here is where the people I love are. That is what 'homeland' means to me.' Otto stood up and went to open a window again. 'It's too hot to have them closed. We will just have to endure the children's noise.'

Wilhelm persisted, 'So do you also think it is all right for all the Jews living in Germany to be calling it their "homeland"?'

'Of course it is! They have lived there for generations. In fact, I rather think they are now almost the only people left in Germany who feel about the world as I do.'

'Hans tells me that some people over there are growing rather suspicious about the Jews – they say they are putting good Germans out of work.'

Emily came in with a tray of coffee and put it near them. She looked up sharply as out in the street there was a sudden noise of a scuffle. Someone shouted, 'I'm goin' ter kill the Kaiser!'

Otto said, 'And as you can hear – some people think that's exactly what we Germans are doing over here.' Emily smiled ruefully at him, and went back to help her mother.

'Will, United Germany is made up of people from many different nations, from Bavaria, Saxony, Prussia, Hanover, even France – Jewish families are just another nation who have been living among their fellow Germans for many generations, and they have enriched the national cultural life immeasurably. Jewish intellectuals were at the heart of the best time to be living in Germany – the Enlightenment – when science and art and new ideas were at the heart of our cultural life. For me they are the good Germans. But long before your mother and I left, all that was disappearing. Big industry combined with military parades and nationalistic banner waving is how a Prussian-dominated Germany wishes to present itself to the world today.'

'So you will never go back to Germany?'

'I don't suppose we ever will. But your mother will always stay in touch with her sister and your cousins. And if it weren't for the present troubles in Servia and the danger that presents, we would be very happy for you to go back with Hans and meet the rest of the family. One day I hope you may. But for us – where our children and grandchildren are, where I can teach and play music – this is homeland enough.'

They drank the coffee in silence and then Otto said, 'The Kaiser thinks he has the right to dominate all the smaller, weaker countries of Europe. Germany now has an immense army and navy, and he wants to use them. These are the dangerous ideas that Germany should worry about. Not the Jews.' He paused. 'I think I must open another window, Wilhelm. I can hardly breathe. Or shall we go out into the garden for a few moments?'

Hans came downstairs with a letter in his hand, and not finding them in the drawing room, followed them outside through the back door.

'Freddie has gone to bed,' he said. 'My father's letter tells me that there is great excitement in Germany about this Servian business and some newspapers are suggesting that von Tirpitz should quickly sort the whole matter out by sending in the German navy.'

'Let's hope not,' said Otto quietly.

Anna turned down the gas, leaving the kitchen in darkness, and she and Emily went through the dimly lit hall to the drawing room. Finding that the men were all still outside, Anna sat down at the piano and began to play the Moonlight Sonata. Otto and William came back in and stood behind her, reading the music over her shoulder, while Hans joined Emily on the sofa and whispered, 'Is Freddie alright, do you think? He was very quiet tonight.'

'Oh! Freddie! He has become as secretive as a fish. I think it's because he's becoming anxious about our German name.' She looked at him. 'Sorry. I am sure it is only because of the newspapers that so many people here have suddenly decided they don't like Germans. It was never like this when we were younger.'

Hans digested this information without saying anything for a minute. Then he said, 'And you? Do you object to belonging to a German family? I know you like to keep it a secret at your college.'

Emily smiled, 'It's just that I prefer that people at College don't know that our parents are German. I – we all – love having you here, Hans. It's nothing to do with that.'

'And Freddie feels the same?'

'Well, I just think he wishes he hadn't told everyone.'

Anna said, 'Wilhelm, before you go you will please write down for me the names and ages of all your boys. I remember Molly's age, but I get into a complete muddle with so many boys. And it is so long since I have seen any of them. How old is your youngest now?'

'Sam? He is six – no seven months.'

*

For the next week still nothing was heard from Gerard Bel-ringer. Hans made a quick return to the Lake District to collect the rest of his equipment and clothes from the farmer, and then came back and remained in Liverpool. In the evenings he made more sketches of Emily, as well as small portraits of Alice, Freddie and his aunt and uncle, and by day he would wander about the streets of Liverpool, drawing the markets, some new buildings going up by the river, and the great new Cathedral in the process of being built at the end of Hope Street. He wrote to his father to ask him to send him his identity papers in case these would now be needed for his journey home.

A postcard with a German stamp arrived for Alice on 16 July.

'I am sorry to have been delayed for so long. Please ask your brother and sister and Hans to come and stay with you to keep you and Miranda company. I hope to be home long before the end of the month. I have got some papers for Hans. G.'

Letter from Gerard Belringer to Alice

The next day the three young people each packed a suitcase and were preparing to set off to take the tram across to West Derby when Gerard Belringer's car appeared outside and the chauffeur knocked at the front door. All anxiety was banished as Emily sat in the front and Hans and Freddie climbed up onto the back of the car, laughing with surprise and excitement.

'I have never dreamed of such a thing! I cannot wait to tell my father. He has never done this, although he always says that the motor car is the great idea of the future. But here we all are. And it is only today!' said Hans. Emily turned and pulled a face at him.

They were driven off by the expressionless chauffeur to stay in Gerard Belringer's new home that he'd had built for himself and Alice on the outskirts of Liverpool, a modern mansion house surrounded by a small park. Otto and Anna stood in the street waving them off until they were out of sight, then they both sighed as they went back indoors.

*

The Austro-Hungarian government has sent an ultimatum to Servia demanding that the following declaration be published on the front page of Servia's official newspaper within 48 hours:

'The Royal Servian Government condemns the propaganda directed against Austria-Hungary, i.e. the entirety of those machinations whose aim it is to separate from the Austro-Hungarian monarchy territories belonging thereto, and she regrets sincerely the ghastly consequences of these criminal actions.

The Royal Servian Government regrets that Servian officers and officials have participated in the propaganda, cited above, and have thus threatened the friendly and neighbourly relations which the Royal Government was solemnly bound to cultivate by its declaration of March 31ˢᵗ 1909.'

Liverpool Echo, 23 July 1914

It was the hottest summer anyone could remember. Liverpool was sweltering and most people were still too busy trying to keep cool to react to the dark portents the newspapers were hinting at. For Otto, however, those reports during those last days of July made very grim reading indeed. By 27 July every European newspaper was full of angry commentaries on Austria's latest *Ultimatum* to Servia, nearly all of them commenting that Germany was certainly behind it.

Anna came through into the kitchen to find Otto reading his paper and looking anxious. 'Oh Otto! You must stop worrying so much about it all. It can't be good for you. Why do the newspapers always blame the Kaiser for everything? You told me he is away on his holiday. Do you really think they are all going to fight a war just because Austria and Servia can't agree about who murdered the poor Archduke?'

'But really,' Otto put his newspaper down, 'No. I still can't believe that this will come to anything more than aggressive sabre rattling. I certainly hope it won't.'

8

Enemy Aliens

'A dark day has today broken over Germany. Envious persons are everywhere compelling us to defence. The sword is being forced into our hand. I hope that, if at the last hour my efforts to bring our adversaries to see things in their proper light and to maintain peace do not succeed, we shall with God's help wield the sword in such a way that we can sheathe it with honour.'

Kaiser Wilhelm II, 31 July

Liverpool – Friday 31 July 1914

Hans went along to the German bank in the centre of Liverpool to collect the money his father had wired him for his journey home.

'The bank is closed,' he told them as he arrived at Otto and Anna's house. 'There's a notice on the outside: "We regret that until further notice all money from Germany has been frozen".'

'Whatever can it mean?' asked Anna.

'It means that Hans must somehow get home, Anna. We shall lend him the money. Your brother-in-law can repay us later.'

'But.... Surely Hans will be perfectly safe as long as he stays here with Gerard? How are you liking living in West Derby, Hans?'

Hans beamed at her. 'Oh it is very good. We are living like lords and ladies with many cooks and chambermaids and chauffeurs. Gerard's house is new and everything is very modern. He has some wonderful impressionist paintings – you have seen them? His latest acquisition is a painting by a lady called Gwen John of a girl reading a letter, and it is so simple and so beautiful it brings tears to my eyes just to look at it. I am very sad that I have to leave now. It has been a great pleasure for me to stay here with you all and get to know my cousins.'

Anna said, 'I hope you are not all being too much trouble for Alice. She is not used to having so many to look after.'

'Oh – but there is a maid and a cook to look after us, so we are all being very spoiled! It was all arranged by Gerard – Alice says she couldn't believe it when these two nice ladies arrived and said they had been sent by Gerard's office. However, I find that we have all easily and instantly become used to being waited on. I am afraid my mother will find me quite impossibly spoilt when I get home!'

Otto said, 'Is there still no news of Gerard?'

'Alice says he will be home very soon now. She has had a letter.'

'We will all be very relieved.'

When Hans had left them, Otto said, 'He must go back at once. Hans says that he has already been called up for military service in Germany as soon as he gets home. If he is registered to serve in the army, then he could be held here as a prisoner of war.'

*

Liverpool – Tuesday 4 August

'Very good, Claire. Much better. Can you feel the difference now?'

Claire nodded grimly as she continued playing with intense concentration, lifting her long thin fingers up off each key as fast as she could.

Otto had recently adopted a new teaching system that had been developed by Tobias Matthay, a German musician living in London. Many musicians suffered from pain and lasting injury as a result of the strain demanded of their hands when they pressed hard down on the keys. Matthay taught a new way of fingering, touching the keys of the piano very lightly to help the displacement of tension, known as 'the German system'. Many of the leading pianists of the day were now going to Matthay for advice. Otto had met him in the autumn of 1913, when he had accompanied Edward Golding to the Royal College of Music for his audition.

The two men had liked one another immediately, and Otto had become so engrossed in his conversation with the tall, balding Professor that he and Edward had nearly missed their train back to Liverpool. Otto was very attracted to Matthay's ideas about the natural laws of music – something which he had often thought about himself – and Matthay had helped him to clarify his own thinking: that it was the velocity of the key that determined the sound of the note, the mere act of touching, combined with the use of the pedal – not the weight or pressure applied to hold the keys down with one's fingers.

Claire Mullins was one of Otto's new pupils for whom he had thought the new German system would be especially helpful. Claire, although she was very dutiful and assiduous and had ability, was temperamentally tense. She was a thin, quiet, shy young woman who wore her fair hair in a long single braid which Otto would tug with mock ferocity when she made mistakes.

'No, no, Claire. You are now putting far too much effort into removing your hands from the keys!'

Claire was obediently repositioning her hands when there was a loud crash. The window above the piano showered shattered glass all over them both. Sliding across the floor until it hit the far wall was a large brick.

They both leapt to their feet, momentarily speechless with shock.

'Are you all right, my dear? Whoever would do such a thing?' Otto spoke eventually.

'I don't know. I don't know. I feel sick.'

'I am so sorry. I am afraid you had better go home now, my dear. I am very sorry that such a shocking thing has happened in the middle of your lesson. Are you feeling all right to make your own way home?'

Claire nodded and shook her head, looking confused.

'Of course there will be no question of you paying for to-day. Please tell your mother. Perhaps I have spent rather too much time teaching you this new fingering method, but if we persevere, I know it will help you in the long run. Next week we shall return to work on your exam piece.' He led her out through the hall to the front door and watched as she walked down the street.

'The English are all humbugs and hypocrites,' Anna announced fiercely when he came back to the music room, where she was busy clearing up the broken shards of glass. 'Haven't I always said so?'

That evening newspaper headline alarmed them both:

August 4: England declares war on Germany

German nationals are all required to register as 'enemy aliens'.

Liverpool – Wednesday 5 August

Early the following morning, Otto and Anna went along to the local police station. Hans had arrived at their house to stay with them the previous night and came along so that they could all register together. After Otto had reported the attack through their window of the day before, he explained to the police sergeant at the desk that they also wanted to register. He and his wife had arrived to live in England thirty years previously as young adults, had remained ever since, and three of their four children and all their grandchildren were British citizens who had been born here, and they now considered their whole family to be British.

'That will be all right, Mr Lohmann,' the policeman at the desk said politely. 'Families like yours are not who the authorities are looking for.'

'But someone has thrown a brick through our window!' Anna's voice went high with outrage.

'And this is our nephew, Hans,' Otto continued quietly. 'My wife's sister's son. He came to visit us from Germany. He is an art student, and has been staying with us since the beginning of July on a painting holiday. Naturally he now must return home as soon as possible.'

'Does he have his papers with him?'

Otto turned to smile at Hans standing behind them, looking very young and nervous. Hans answered for himself, 'I believed I did not need a pass to come to England for a holiday.'

Otto turned back to the policeman. 'His papers are being sent over for him, but unfortunately they haven't yet arrived. However, my wife and I can vouch for him.'

'I'm sorry, Sir, but I have had orders to take into protective custody any German nationals who are here without proof of identity or means of support.'

'But he is our nephew!' Anna burst in. 'He is a young boy. We are his proof of identity. And he has means of support, because he is our guest. He is staying with our son-in-law, Mr Belringer, who is highly respected by the government. This is all humbug!'

Otto held her dramatically waving hands and spoke calmly to the sergeant. 'Protective custody – what does that mean? As he intends to return home to Germany as soon as his documents arrive, may he not remain in our protective custody until then?'

'Would you mind waiting in here while I go and consult my superior officer?'

They were shown into a bare room with twenty or more chairs against the walls, and sat down to wait. Otto was frowning.

Anna said, 'It is almost as if we were the criminals, when our house has been attacked by vandals. You would think they would ask about that.'

'Let's just all keep calm and wait and see what they have to say,' said Otto.

Ten minutes later the desk sergeant came back to say the Chief Inspector would see them in his office. The front desk was now crowded with anxious-looking men and a long queue stretched on outside the building. Otto, Anna and Hans were led through to the back of the station. The Sergeant knocked on a door and they were shown into a large room where a big red-haired man was seated behind a desk. A notice in front of them proclaimed that this was Chief Inspector O'Brien. He looked up and indicated the chairs they should sit on. He nodded to the Sergeant, who left the room.

'I understand you have lived in this country for many years, Mr –er – Lawman?'

'Lohmann. Yes. My wife and I came to live here in 1875 and Liverpool has long been our home. We have two sons and two daughters and all but our eldest son were born in England and have British nationality. My eldest son and eldest daughter are both married to English people, and have children. My other son and daughter are both still students. Our nephew here, who has come to visit us, is an art student and has been painting in the Lake District, and is on the point of departure back to Germany. He has asked his father to send over his documents, but they have not arrived so far.'

'Well, Sir, once you and your wife have registered with us, there will be no further action taken. My sergeant tells me you work for the Liverpool council. The only difficulty is your nephew. I understand you are here without any papers, young man?'

'They are on the way. When I arrived there was no question of needing any. I only came here to visit my uncle and aunt for a painting holiday.'

'Then I am afraid that, for your own safety, we are going to have to keep you here until we can find the means of having you transported back to Germany. Officially, I am afraid you are now officially an enemy alien with no papers.'

Anna burst in, 'Transported! Oh this is wonderful. Enemy alien! A boy on a painting holiday! Well, if you are going to "transport" him, perhaps you would like to come to our home and pack his trunk for him! You can mend our broken window and collect your brick at the same time. I see you have nothing to say about that!'

'Anna! Be silent.'

'I will not be silent. This is an outrage.'

'I am very sorry, Madam. I do understand how difficult this is for you. Feelings are running high at the moment. If you wish you may bring a small suitcase of your nephew's clothes and toilet things down here to the station.'

'Surely he can stay with us until his father sends over his documents?'

The policeman sighed impatiently. 'As I said, for your nephew's own safety he must remain at the police station until we have further instructions. Now you must excuse me – I have a great deal to do.' He stood up, towering over them, making it clear the interview was over. 'We are only going to hold people here for a very short time, until they can be repatriated or, in a very few cases, they may be taken on to more permanent ac-commodation. Your nephew will be treated very well, I do assure you. And once he has his papers, he can be repatriated.'

He shepherded them out of his office.

The streets outside the police station were full of confusion and noise. People were yelling and shouting at one another. They had to push their way through crowds of people, some shouting crude anti-German slogans.

Gerard Belringer reappeared the next morning and Otto told him what had happened to Hans. 'Damn and blast. I was afraid of that. Well – at least I now have his papers with me – I went and spoke to his father while I was over there and collected them – just in case. Leave it to me. I'll sort it out. But I'm afraid it may take a week or two. He'll be perfectly all right where he is for now.'

'You've been to Berlin?'

'Briefly.'

'Well if you can do anything at all, Gerard – as you can imagine, we are very upset about this.'

Ten days later they received a postcard from Hans, who said he had been kept at the police station for a week but was now interned in a large empty mill on the outskirts of Manchester with several hundred others in the same position. He wrote that he was fine and they were not to worry. In a longer letter two days later he wrote that Otto might even quite like it there, as some of the internees were musicians and had even brought their instruments. And there was another man who had simply been in England on a painting holiday, like himself.

Over the next two weeks the streets of Liverpool were quiet, although still tense and hostile. Children were kept indoors. Many German employees had been sacked from their jobs, and all of them were now being rounded up and detained. Otto and Anna escaped any more direct assaults but, one by one, Otto's pupils all began cancelling their lessons.

'Promise me,' Otto said to Mrs Mullins, when she called round to the house to tell him that her daughter, Claire, would no longer be coming to him, 'that she won't lose her love of music. When she plays from the heart, she plays like an angel. If she plays from her head only, something will always be missing. I am sorry indeed not to be able to finish preparing her for her grade 7.'

'Why don't you take your family back home to Germany, Professor Lohmann?' Mrs Mullins said. Otto bowed his head and showed her to the door without replying.

Liverpool – September 1914

Gerard Belringer arrived one afternoon and asked to speak to Otto alone. They went out into the garden and stood face to face in Otto's greenhouse, Anna staring curiously through her kitchen window at the two silhouettes. Gerard told Otto that Hans was on his way to America.

'America!'

'I'm only sorry it has taken me so long – if only I'd got home a day or two earlier, none of this needed to happen. One thing that delayed me was that I had to make a detour into Berlin in order to collect Hans' papers – I knew he would need them. His father confided in me that they were rather unhappy about him coming home now because he would have to go straight into the army. Their other sons are professional soldiers, but his mother doesn't believe that Hans would be able to cope with army life. So as it turns out – this is better. I have arranged for him to go with some cargo I am shipping to the States.'

'But however did you manage to get his release, Gerard?'

'Well – I had his identification papers, and I used my political connections rather shamelessly. Luckily we have a Liberal government. And the Governor actually seemed quite glad to let him go – the numbers they are holding are mounting up and they are having problems accommodating them all. The main thing is that Hans will soon be safely in America and needn't get involved if there is to be a long war. He will stay with some friends of mine over there.'

'His parents will be so relieved. And Anna will be beside herself with joy. We can't thank you enough, Gerard.'

'Yes. But I am afraid I am still a bit concerned – and this is why I wanted to speak to you alone, Otto. I don't want to alarm Anna any more than I have to. They are talking of building a camp for at least 5,000 internees on the Isle of Man and the police are now asking for authority to intern anyone with any connection at all with Germany. Even highly respected people like yourself may yet be interned if the war escalates any further.'

'But surely it won't? We were very much hoping it would all end very quickly.'

'I am afraid the only way that can happen is if Germany is allowed to win the war. They are so far advanced militarily they are completely unstoppable. I doubt the allies, even all working together, are a match for them – certainly not in the short term. So I am afraid that you must be prepared for the possibility of you and William also being interned. I am so sorry to say it and I will do everything in my power to prevent it. But William must be warned. If I hear anything, I will let you know at once. I will do my best.'

Otto was struck by how Gerard, always so youthful looking, suddenly seemed much older. The two men shook hands, and after kissing Anna briefly on his way through the house and refusing all offers of hospitality, Gerard left as swiftly as he had arrived.

Liverpool – Christmas 1914

Things remained quiet in the city over Christmas 1914. Unregistered German and Austrian nationals were still being rounded up, but those who had lived in the country for a number of years or had valid business reasons for being in Britain, as long as they had registered, were left in peace. Otto talked to William about Gerard's warning, but William didn't believe that there could be any possible danger for him, with his growing family of English children. He was now the senior salesman of his publishing company, which had expanded to publish classic children's fiction in addition to its successful and ever increasing core list of popular fiction about working class life in the north.

Christmas came and went; the war just kept on going.

9

'Lusitania'

Liverpool – January 1915

At the end of January, Leah and Will's seventh son was born. They called him Frederick, after his uncle. Leah was by now so experienced that the midwife left her sitting up in bed, her faced washed and hair brushed, her baby swaddled and clean in his cradle beside her, within an hour of the delivery.

'You are not to get out of bed for any reason at all, Mrs Lohmann,' the midwife said sternly as she left. 'You must ask your husband if you need anything. I'll be back this evening to make sure all is well and to help you with your toilet.'

'I'll be fine, Fran. We both will. I'm not even tired. Thank you for taking such good care of us, as you always do. Ask Will to come up to meet his new son now, would you?'

*

Friday 7 May 1915

'Lusitania' *Torpedoed by Enemy Submarine*

The famous Cunard liner, 'Lusitania', was torpedoed as it arrived in Irish waters shortly after two o'clock today by a German submarine. There were 1,313 passengers aboard and 665

crew. 703 were rescued, but many of these died soon after-
wards of shock and exposure. The passengers and crew were
all non-combatants.

Liverpool Echo, 7 May

William was back in Liverpool on the eighth of May with his
department boss for a meeting with Sir Ronald Golding, the
owner of their publishing house, who wanted to talk to them
about newly published material by OUP explaining the background to the events leading up to Britain's declaration of war
now. Sir Ronald had the idea that one of their own authors
might be able to write a 'popular' book explaining the reasons
for joining the war for their own market. William's boss wasn't
sure if it would be wise to diversify so far from their reputation
for popular fiction publishing.

After the meeting William went round to his parents' house.
He came in round the back and found them both in the kitchen.
Anna was ironing and Otto was sitting at the table reading
aloud from a London newspaper. He glanced up as William
came smiling in through the back door, told him to sit down
and listen, then continued reading:

'... There is no crime which Germany will shrink from
committing. Indignation is no deterrent. The Kaiser may be a

homicidal maniac like Jack the Ripper, but he has got an organised nation of 65 millions behind his blood-lust. This nation of barbarians possesses all the resources of modern science. It will use them all without scruple. Land-murder and sea-murder are not the end. They are the beginning.

The Germans have poisoned wells in South Africa. They will go farther than well-poisoning in Europe. What moral force will restrain them? I can think of none. They will mobilise their chemists and their bacteriologists. Rather than accept defeat they will spread pestilence and plague in France, in Russian, and in the United Kingdom. The wild beasts who sank the Lusitania *are capable of using plague cultures as a weapon of war.'*

Article in *Star*

Otto looked up from his paper to see the effect the report was having on them, his own eyes full of tears. William was shaking his head 'I know. I know. It's awful.'

Otto said, 'William. I'm glad you've come. We shall all have to decide what to do about this – just listen.'

He looked up at them both to make sure they were listening, before reading:

'All enemy aliens must be interned in camps. That is the elementary precaution which we must adopt. There are many others which men of science can think out.'

Anna was nearly hysterical with fright. 'What can it mean?'

'This article has been printed in all the national papers,' said Otto. 'We must keep calm, but we must face facts. It might come to Will and me both being detained.'

Will shook his head. 'Oh no, Father. Surely not. Everybody knows us. You and Mother have lived here for years, it's your home, and I was practically born here. They cannot possibly mean to arrest us. This is just some hysterical journalist. I now have seven English sons and a daughter and a Welsh wife.'

'Oh yes, Wilhelm. How is dear Leah?' Anna's mind flew with relief to the more interesting topic. 'Is she well? How is the baby?'

'Yes, she is very well. She is always happy when she has a new baby to look after.' He smiled at them. 'We are calling him Freddy – like his uncle.'

Otto looked up from his newspaper, 'You might come to regret having another mouth to feed, William. What happens to your family now, if we are interned?'

'We won't be, Father. We registered immediately it was called for. This is our home now. We are all British citizens.' He picked up the newspaper and glanced at it with contempt.

'These journalists love to make things sound much worse than they are. The meeting I was at today was very interesting about what is really happening. Sir Ronald wants us to publish a book explaining all the background so people can understand. There is still a lot of diplomatic work going on behind the scenes.'

'England is our home, but British citizens we are not,' Otto reminded him.

William yawned suddenly, and then apologised. 'It's been a long day. I would be so grateful, Mama, if we could eat fairly soon so I can be early to my bed. I have to get back to Manchester first thing tomorrow.'

Later that evening a large looming figure with whistles, badges and torches slung about his dark uniform appeared in the dusk and knocked loudly on the front door. PC Barton was a member of the Liverpool Choral Society, and had sung in the Messiah with William and Leah before they moved away to Manchester. Otto had given his youngest daughter piano lessons for a short time, when her regular teacher was having a baby.

'Good evening, Professor,' he said to Otto at the front door. 'May I come in?' Otto held back the heavy draft curtain for him. Once indoors, the policeman looked uncomfortably big in the dimly-lit hallway. He spoke formally.

'Professor Lohmann, I have been ordered to tell you that you are to report to the local police station tomorrow morning, with a small suitcase packed and ready for internment....' He paused to allow Otto time to take it in. 'I am so very sorry about this, Professor. It's the new regulations.'

William and Anna both appeared in the kitchen doorway behind Otto, their faces frozen in identical expressions of anxious curiosity.

'Packed? Does that mean that I will not be returning home between reporting at the police station and internment?' Otto spoke quietly and calmly.

'From the police station you will be taken directly to a holding centre. It is for the authorities there to decide what happens next. It is for your own protection. There has been a lot of disturbance since the war began. And especially now ... well, as you know, the *'Lusitania'* was a Liverpool ship and ...'

He paused when he saw Wilhelm. 'Oh! Good evening, Will. This may mean you, too, I'm afraid. I don't know how the Manchester force is organising things, but they will have had similar orders to ours.'

Anna nearly shouted, 'But my son has lived here since he was a babe in arms. He can't even speak German – how can you possibly want – and he has eight children! What is to become of them if you take away their father, the family bread-winner? You tell me that. You know him. Oh, please, please, don't do this terrible thing.'

Wilhelm said nothing but made a strange sound. Turning round to look at him, Otto wondered for a moment whether his son was going to laugh. He had a frozen expression, with a fixed grin and his eyebrows lifted. Otto turned back to the policeman.

'Of course we all understand that you have to do your duty, Constable Barton. I will be there. But cannot we be given a little more time to prepare ourselves? We need to make provision for our loved ones if we are to be held for a long time.'

'I hope it will all be over very soon, Professor.'

'We all hope that.'

'You will need to bring your identification documents – your birth certificate and a passport or identity card if you have one.'

'I have no passport,' said Otto. 'We have never needed one. Even before we came to make England our home,' he emphasised the last word, 'I could travel all over Europe without ever needing such a thing.'

'I have a passport,' said William suddenly. He looked at his father. 'I thought I'd need one if I was going back with Ha....' Otto interrupted him quickly, 'I'm sure Sir Ronald won't be sending you to France now, William. There's too much uncertainty.'

'You were about to travel abroad, Will?'

'Well, I was just … but my father is right – it is very unlikely now.'

'I shouldn't mention that to anyone else if I were you, Will.'

When the police constable left they went back into the kitchen. Otto sat down, suddenly exhausted, put his hands on the edge of the table and closed his eyes. Anna went upstairs, and after a few minutes he went up to see what she was doing. She had pulled his clothes out of the wardrobe and they were lying in a small heap on the bed. Anna was kneeling beside it, weeping. Otto knelt beside her, and put his arms around her. She clung to him, sobbing.

'Oh please, Anna, don't,' said Otto after a while. 'I can't bear it.'

'But what's to become of you, and what's to become of me and Leah and the boys, and the rest of the family? Oh what's to become of us all?'

'You will cope – as you have bravely done before through so many difficult times, Anina. You are my wonderful, brave girl.'

Anna's voice was shrill. 'They said last year when it all started – it would all be over by Christmas. And now look! I think this will go on forever.'

'Calmness, Anna. Courage. Come downstairs now. We must talk to William – he will be wondering what has happened to us. We must all decide together what has to be done.'

Downstairs, they sat round the kitchen table. William had made a pot of tea. Otto said, 'It doesn't matter about me. The important thing is to try to save William. What we need to do is discover whether there is any reprieve for people who can prove they have no connection with Germany and who are German only by birth. Carl Schindler's son has joined up in the British Army. You must contact Gerard tomorrow, and see if he can help. I am sure they will think twice about keeping you, William, even if they have to detain me. When we get to the holding centre there may well be a hearing that you can attend. They can't possibly mean to intern us all. There are thousands of Germans living in Liverpool alone. Where would they put us all? Please don't upset yourself, dearest Anna. All will be well.'

'Britain Awake!'

What has awakened Britain? The sinking of the Lusitania. *It simply cannot be explained away. In her heart, Britain knows that soothing syrup and soft sawder are useless....*

If anyone had predicted last July that the Germans would poison wells, would employ chemical poisons to inflict terrible agony on our soldiers, and would butcher women and children on a Cunard liner, he would have been derided. These fiends are not bound by any law of God or man....

We must take no chances with the Imperial madman and his hordes of maniacs. Let us sit down and take steps to meet any possible development of frightfulness....

We ought instantly to close all our ports against aliens, and especially against aliens from the United States. If the weapon of pestilence is used against us, we may be sure that the blow will be struck by miscreants from America. The appalling venom of the hyphenated American is hardly realised by the British people. It rages openly in their hyphenated journals. When Herr Dernburg was asked by American reporters what Americans would think of the Lusitania *horror, he brutally retorted, 'Let them think!' Forewarned is forearmed....*

Let us remember that the war-doctrine of the German Emperor and his organised murder-bureau is that the end justifies any means. Rather than be crushed, the Kaiser will try to destroy civilisation....

The Lusitania *has settled that once and for all. We must organise our virility as it has never been organised in our history. We must organise it not for months, but for years ahead.*

James Douglas, *London Opinion*, 22 May 1915

10

Knockaloe

Regarding the holding of aliens, I think it must be the 'alien clique' of boarding house keepers who want to take them in, as I am sure no-one with a touch of Manx blood in them would think of taking such trash in; they would rather starve first. If only they could see our poor fellows coming down wounded and gassed, they wouldn't have much time for boarding Germans, I'm sure. The best place for them would be in pig-styes. I have often stood in front of a German band with an orange in my hand, sucking it, but I have got something harder for them now, I assure you. Keep them away from our boarding houses, because no decent person will want to stay in a house that any of these beasts have stayed in. I have spoken to Belgians and they have told me of some of the German doings.

Letter to the Isle of Man Weekly Times,
26 June 1915, from Sergeant Radcliffe ASC

Liverpool – June 1915

A week after the sinking of the great liner so close to its home port, Otto and William were imprisoned with 200 others in the same holding camp outside Manchester where Hans had been taken a year earlier. Three of their fellow internees were members of the Manchester Halle Orchestra, including their conductor, Hans Richter. They all believed that they would be able to resume their normal lives once the uproar over the sinking of the *Lusitania* had died down. One of them whom Otto knew said, 'What would happen to Sir Edward's music if we are all kept prisoners in here indefinitely?'

Liverpool – October 1915

Four months later, Otto, William and about 70 others were taken by an evening train back to Liverpool and marched down to Liverpool docks. In spite of the lateness of the hour, a crowd of jeering bystanders was waiting at the quayside. The prisoners were pelted with rotten eggs and vegetable peelings before they were put aboard a steamer at Liverpool pier head, to be taken across to Douglas, on the Isle of Man.

Isle of Man – October 1915

Otto woke up with a start, feeling sick. A swaying motion underneath him made his stomach come up to his throat. There was a strong smell of fish. His neck felt dislocated and he was freezing cold. For a few seconds he had no idea where he was. He opened his eyes, adjusted his head on the old canvas bag that he had been using for a pillow, felt for his spectacles and peered around. It was no dream. The others were all there, mostly still asleep, stretched out in various positions of discomfort on the floor of the deck. He looked around for William. He seemed to have managed to create a little tent out of his raincoat with its corduroy collar and was almost hidden underneath it.

Otto struggled to his feet and staggered to the nearest window. Outside, the dim grey dawn light showed just enough headland to reveal that they were sailing backwards, the water slapping noisily against the sides of the wallowing ferry. A dark figure, rifle slung sloppily over his shoulder, was leaning on the rail smoking a cigarette. He remembered that other steamer, years ago, when they had all come over from Hamburg, and he too had leaned on the rail smoking, peering entranced into the magical darkness of the North Sea night. He tapped on the window but the figure ignored him, flicked the cigarette end overboard and moved away.

The boat backed slowly up to a dark pier. A few arc lights provided the only colour in a monochrome world. The prisoners were roused politely and with some sympathy by the crew who were unaccustomed to having their boat used as a dormitory, especially by people like all these well-dressed and in many cases quite elderly men.

Otto and William joined the others in a bewildered queue shuffling out through the saloon doors onto the deck. Two soldiers and a policeman stood by the doorway and pushed them through. The policeman was looking intently at each man as he passed.

'What do you make it?'

'76.'

'I got 75. I'm not counting them all again. Put 75. Let the Camp sort it out.'

The policeman wrote the number in a little black book. He called out to someone in the morning darkness, 'Mr Gormley! Another 75 for Knockaloe!'

The two soldiers directed them down the gang-plank to the wharf at Douglas. From Douglas pier they were marched to the station and taken by train across to Knockaloe, where a huge camp had been constructed on the west coast of the island.

Knockaloe camp was still in process of being built across a wide moor, eventually covering 22 acres, divided into four camps. A specially constructed rail-link brought in food and provisions. At the beginning of the first year everyone had slept in tents, but by the time Otto and Will arrived the internees were living in newly constructed rows of wooden huts. Originally intended for only 5,000 internees, now, largely because of the increase in violent hostility towards all Germans after the sinking of the *Lusitania*, there were 15,000 men, and huts were being built for the even greater number still expected.

Liverpool – November 1915

Ach mein Schatzerl! Zuerst lass mich Dich beruhigen – Wilhelm und Ich sind bei einander, und werden richtig behandelt. Nichts zu fürchten unsertwegen. Bitte schreib uns: c/o Camp 4, Knockaloe, Isle of Man. Ich habe fest gestellt dass Briefe erlaubt sind, von und nach Hause, dazu auch bekommen wir £1 pro Woche. Doch etwas. Wir sollen Gerard vertrauen, dass er Leah und den Kindern hilft – sicher wird er sie nicht hungern lassen. Sei mutig meine Liebste.

Dein Otto.

(Postcard from Knockaloe from Otto to Anna)

Anna read the card aloud to Freddie and Emily, who looked frightened as if they only half understood. Anna translated it for them:

Oh my sweetheart. First let me put your mind at rest – Will and I are both here together, we are being treated correctly and there is nothing to fear on our behalf. You can now write to us c/o Camp 3, Knockaloe, I. of Man. I have ascertained that we can receive and write letters home and I may send you £1 a week. It is something. We must put our trust in Gerard to help

131

you and Leah and the children – I am certain he will not let
you starve. Be brave, my dearest.

Your Otto.

'Is there nothing we can do, Mother?' Emily was tearful.
'Father is an old man. He's not well.'

'He wants us all to be very brave. We will all write to him
at once, so he knows that we are keeping cheerful and well. He
mustn't have the extra burden of worrying about us.'

'It is so unjust. Only a year ago he was being celebrated.
And now this!'

'He will always be celebrated in this house. Come – we
must not show the world long faces. We can hold our heads
high. We have done nothing to be ashamed of. It is the English
who should be ashamed. But for now, we must do all we can to
help Leah and the children until our beloved ones are safely
home again.'

*

Knockaloe – October 1916
There had been a diphtheria outbreak in Manchester. Anyone
who contracted it had to be held in quarantine. William
received a letter from Leah with terrible news. Their little girl,
Molly, had contracted it. She was only five years old, but Leah
had been forced to take her to a sanatorium and leave her there
with strangers. Molly had always been a very strong little girl –

132

she had to be, growing up with so many big brothers – and Leah had felt sure she would recover. But Molly had died in the sanatorium, on her own.

William found Otto sitting at the piano in the recreation hall, alone and silent.

'Father?'

Otto looked up slowly and stared at his son. William could see that Otto had heard the news.

'I was so sure. I was so *sure* that the world outside Germany was more enlightened, more open. I knew Germany was becoming nationalistic and unwelcoming to liberal ideas. I persuaded your mother to come with me to live over here. I believed that I was bringing her – and you, Will, and my young sisters – all of you – to a better life, where we could all become part of a more enlightened world. But now here we are – enemy aliens in our own country, our loved ones struggling to survive. And now our granddaughter – your brave little Molly – Oh Will, I'm sorry. I can't bear it.' He began to weep.

William shook his head and looked away. Neither man spoke for a while. Then William said, 'Whoever's fault it is, Father, it certainly isn't yours. I have to accept that my darling Molly would have died, even if I had been there. There was nothing anyone could have done. And as for everything else, well – I had almost forgotten I was German. But since being here, seeing how everybody is coping with this life, has made me feel proud to be one of them. They are artists. They are teachers. You can't become a musician or teacher or artist without being able to feel and imagine. You must have a generous spirit. I have found that spirit here. Of course I love England too, but here I feel quite proud that we are German.'

'Oh yes. Here there are many exceptional men who happen to be German. But it is also no surprise that these are so many of the ones who *are* here. The exceptional ones do not feel comfortable in Germany, and they have left to come to live in Britain or France or America.... I now wish I had done what my dear Anna wanted and taken us all on to America. But I took a liking to this country. To Liverpool especially. I like the people. But how are we ever going to be able to face all our old friends and neighbours again, knowing how much they must hate us? They hate our whole nation because it has allowed itself to be led astray by one mad, bad German, the Kaiser.'

'Who the hell started this bloody war anyway? And what is anyone supposed to be gaining from it?'

Otto shook his head. 'Land and power. That's all the Kaiser is after. And self-aggrandisement – it is sheer madness.'

'Well, at least I have the comfort of knowing that my boys are all keeping their mother safe and helping her with the youngest ones. I'm so proud of them all. And you and I are safe here.'

'Those of us who have kept quiet have been safe. Not that young man who tried to escape. And some of the guards here may soon come to very much resent the fact that they have to feed us while they have so little to give their own families. War makes even good people cruel.'

The next day Will was out with a working party, and on the way home he heard a sound that made him look up. Flying high above him was a solitary wild goose. There was no sign of any others. He took off his cap and shouted and waved until the bird was out of sight. 'Goodbye, my darling! I will never forget you.'

*

Knockaloe – May 1917

To Edgar

With sincerest Birthday Greetings and all good wishes. Hoping you may now begin to expand into Broadminded Broadshouldered and Broadhearted Manhood.

With Dad's fondest and deepest affection

Knockaloe, 10/5/17

Knockaloe – January 1918

Any communication of the subject of this letter
Should be addressed to:-

The Under Secretary of State

Home Office   HOME OFFICE,

London S.W.1.   WHITEHALL.

8 Jan 1918

Sir,

I am directed by the Secretary of State to inform you that the
application of the under-mentioned alien enemies for
exemption from repatriation has been considered by the
Advisory Committee and it has been decided that these persons
may remain in this country: Otto Lohmann and Wilhelm
Lohmann.

The Secretary of State has also decided that the persons in
question may be released from internment and I am to request
that you will release them forthwith.

I am, Sir,

Your obedient Servant,

John Pedder

The Commandant

*

Liverpool – February 1918

Gerard was there to meet them off the ferry, driving his own car. They all shook hands rather tearfully, and Gerard tried to keep up a flow of unemotional commentary as he drove them to Otto's home, where Anna, Emily and Frederick were waiting outside the front door, looking out for them. As soon as they climbed out of the car, Otto and William embraced a weeping Anna. Alice and her daughter Maisie were also there to greet them, but they left soon afterwards with Gerard, promising to come back the next day.

Otto was shocked to find Anna so thin and pale. William had wept when he had first seen his mother. Even over supper that evening, they hardly spoke except for Anna's occasional involuntary exclamations of joy as she kept clasping Otto and William's hands to reassure herself they were really there. Otto would smile at her, squeeze her hand and shake his head unable to speak with emotion, and William looked as though he was about to weep again.

After supper Otto left Anna and William together while he talked first to Emily and then to Frederick separately in his music room. The piano had gone. Emily told him that for the last year Anna had never left the house. She was too proud to ask for help from anyone, even her own children, and had insisted on subsisting entirely on the £1 a week Otto had been allowed to send home.

Emily told Otto how Anna's friend, Muriel Cartwright's eldest son, had been killed in action early in 1916. When Anna had called round to express her sorrow, Muriel's daughter had come to the door, and when she had seen it was Anna, had shut the front door in her face. When Anna heard that Muriel had lost her youngest son on the Western Front in 1917, Anna had wept uncontrollably for days on end. Since then she had never left the house.

Emily had qualified as a teacher and found a job as an assistant in a local school for £1 a week, but Anna insisted that she and Frederick should each give a part of their salary to Leah, and as far as possible to save some of what was left. They had both privately agreed they would supplement the family larder somehow without her knowing. Alice, too, had usually managed to slip some eggs or a little butter into the larder when she came over, and Emily would quickly make a meal for Anna out of them without her knowing, but in spite of this, for most of the time they had all been living on near starvation rations. Emily told Otto how Freddie had kept them all from total despair by always being positive and coming home with stories about the doings and sometimes witty sayings of customers in the chemist shop where he worked, that had managed to take their minds off their troubles.

When Freddie himself came in to see Otto, he seemed upset and shaken.

'I'm so sorry, Father. I know I've let you down.'

'Freddie! What can you mean? Your sister has been telling me how much they both depended on you, and how much you helped keep your mother's spirits up.'

'I sold your piano, Father! I am so sorry. I thought Mother was starving and I just couldn't stand to watch it. She was so angry with me.'

'Of course you did! And how much I thank you for it! How could anyone think that was wrong? Emily says it was your calm fortitude, and your wonderful ability to see humour even in the darkest days that kept them both from despair. I am proud of you and so grateful you were here, my son. And Emily has also told me about all you had to put up with – people shouting at you and demanding to know why you weren't in uniform – but you never complained or worried your mother with it. Believe me, Freddie, you have done all and more than I could have asked or hoped for. Now let's go back and rejoin your mother and sister before you make me cry!'

William stayed at his parents' home for one night, and after another long talk with his mother the next morning, he left for

Manchester by train. Alice arrived soon after William had left. She asked to talk to Otto privately.

'Gerard tried so hard to get you both released, Papa. He had been helping Mr Asquith by giving him information about the size and capability of the Kaiser's navy, and Mr Asquith helped him to arrange to get Hans out. But then there was the awful *Lusitania* business.... '

'It's all right, my dear. I didn't expect him to be able to help us. There were far more important things for him to worry about. As long as you were both able to look after the family at home – that was the only thing that mattered.'

'No, but – Gerard got into terrible trouble. The auditors looking at his accounts discovered that the German U-boat that had attacked and sunk the *Lusitania* was equipped with engine parts from his own Belringer yard. Even though they had been ordered and delivered before the outbreak of war, the final payment didn't arrive until 1915, and his accountants here reported it. The factory was closed down and Gerard was arrested. It got into all the papers.' She looked at her father, who was shaking his head in disbelief.

'Gerard wasn't allowed anywhere near Mr Asquith or to contact him after that – especially when the papers mentioned his having a 'German' wife. And then – well, poor Mr Asquith had a sort of nervous breakdown and Mr Lloyd George took over.... Mr Asquith did eventually meet up with Gerard again and helped him. He spoke to the authorities, who finally accepted that all Gerard's business dealings with Germany had been a cover so that he could keep the British government informed about the size and capacity of the Kaiser's navy. Everyone had known for years that the Kaiser was preparing to invade other countries. Eventually Gerard was allowed home without a trial. But he was held in prison for over a year, and it has meant I could do so little to help our Mother....'

'My poor darling Alice! Why ever didn't any of you tell me about this in your letters? What you must have gone through! Please tell Gerard I am so sorry and I hope he will come and see me soon. I must shake his hand.'

'We thought it would make matters worse if they knew I was writing to you. But now Gerard says that the war will soon be over now the Americans are there. The German army is on its last legs.'

'I only hope he's right, but I can't see the Kaiser ever admitting defeat. At Knockaloe some of our fellow prisoners were still managing to get news from Germany, and they were all convinced they had nearly won the war already.'

'Gerard says both armies are exhausted and at the end of their resources, but now the Americans have joined the allies, it will be only a matter of time.'

Otto hugged his daughter and smiled at her. 'The worst part for me has been feeling so much blame for all the suffering and problems you have all had to bear. All I want to do now is to make it up to you all as much as I can.'

*

By 1918 over 24,000 men had been detained at Knockaloe. Some, like Otto and William, were released during the course of 1918. By the end of 1919 the majority of those still there would be repatriated; a few, providing they could be vouched for by employers, were to be allowed to return to their lives in England.

Officials who visited the camps just after the war was over were horrified by conditions there:

'Round the moorland farm of Knockaloe, there grew rapidly a vast temporary wooden town. No woman or child was to be seen in this town; it contained no cottage or mansion, but a haze of smoke by day and a blaze of electric light at night time showed from afar where lay the ranks of black huts in which its folk were to eat and sleep together for three or four weary years. Outside, the fences of barbed wire and the pacing sentries were an everlasting reminder that the world was at war and that the inhabitants of Knockaloe Camp must keep out of the world until the war was ended.

'The camp was pitched on the eastern slopes of a range of hills, which on their western side run steeply down to the Irish Sea. The summit of the hill cut off the camp from sight of the sea, though from a few of the enclosures one could catch a glimpse of Peel Harbour, almost two miles to the north. On the landward side there was a wide prospect away to Greeba Hill beyond St. John's. Fortunately it became possible for a small number of the prisoners to get out of camp as members of working parties, repairing roads, banking streams, or working on the land, and kindly tales were told of sympathetic farm wives and of children's smiles. But for most of the men such friendly and personal intercourse remained a dream, and to them the outside world was represented by the crowded chara-bancs that drove across from Douglas to "see the Germans " behind their bars, as one might go to the Zoo.'

Official report of conditions at Knockaloe

11

Homecoming

Manchester – February 1918

Leah's letters had not prepared William for what he found when he got home. The two eldest, Albert and Edgar, had both left school before the war, Albert had gone to work in a cotton mill and Edgar was apprenticed to a local engineering company; they also helped at a local farm at the weekends. Leo, at only fourteen, had been taken on as a runner by a local newspaper; Philip and Clifford were both still at school, but had frequently truanted in order to earn money running errands for neighbours and local shopkeepers. Clifford had become very skilled at finding items in the shops that had 'fallen on the floor'. Sam and Freddy were both still at junior school, but all the older boys supplemented their wages by scavenging round nearby fields for turnips, cabbages and potatoes. They were all as thin and undernourished as William and Otto had become during their internment.

Leah had turned the garden borders entirely over to growing vegetables and the lawn was now inside a fence of posts and wire and scratched to bare earth by seven brown hens Leah had managed to raise from some eggs Clifford had found. Two of the eggs had hatched out into cockerels, and these had provided them with last year's Christmas dinner. Most of the time they all lived off soup made from potatoes and turnips and whatever other scraps they had managed to scavenge round the farm. Albert and Edgar had taken 9-year old Tess, their old family dog, back to the farm where she had been raised.

The older boys were thin and brown, and the youngest two, Sam and Freddy, both looked pale and unwell. In 1917 there had been a second outbreak of diphtheria. Four-year-old Sam caught it. This time Leah refused to report it. She locked herself in one room for three months with Sam, stuffed rags and sheets under the door, only coming out at night when the family were all asleep or at work, to get the supplies of food and water the boys left out for her on the kitchen table. Sam had survived. Leah told William she couldn't have borne to have left another child to die alone in the infirmary, but that she had been too terrified to tell William in case the authorities read her letters. William could only shake his head in wonder and dismay.

Everyone was exhausted. William had expected his sons to be overjoyed to see him back as he was to see them. Instead he found the eldest boys were almost hostile, and the two youngest, who had been babies when he left, were shy and awkward with him because to them he was a stranger. Only Leo, Clifford and Philip had greeted him with any show of affection.

While he had been on the Isle of Man, William had somehow managed to find positive experiences out of his incarceration, and had formed friendships with some of his fellow inmates. Even Otto had come to respect the deeply ingrained German work ethic that meant that camp life was organised as far as possible to help everyone spend their time constructively. Anyone who wasn't being sent out to work on the local farms and factories could attend art classes and maths, history or geography lessons organised by the prisoners themselves. There were a number of imprisoned musicians, including Otto, who had put on concerts. It had all helped to make life seem more bearable.

But in spite of all they could do, it had been a time of misery and anxiety for most of them. Sometimes groups of local Islanders would come and stare at the prisoners as though they were animals in a zoo, and hurl abuse at them. The guards resented giving food to the prisoners when they had barely enough to feed their own families, and kept the rations down to a minimum. Gambling became prevalent, which led to crime, sometimes violent, as men tried to retrieve the money they lost. Many suffered from depression and became mentally unstable. Food shortages weakened their resistance to colds and 'flu and disease spread quickly; some died in captivity. There were German and Turkish spies who tried to cause ferment and had been shot. Others were shot when trying to escape.

Hopeless as it was, escape did seem possible – looking to the west from the top of the camp the coast of Ireland appeared tantalisingly close, and if they were taken out to work on the farms, they could clearly see the coast of England to the east. William and Otto had both sometimes found themselves standing and staring hopelessly across towards Liverpool.

It was a long, slow struggle for William to recover from the devastation the war had inflicted on them all. After the initial euphoria of homecoming, feelings of despair had soon overwhelmed him. He knew that even with the boys all working hard, the family was still struggling to make ends meet. Now that he was home, William experienced a painful feeling of separation between his sons and himself. Sam and Freddy had been suspicious and shy with him for a long time after he came back. William had mourned for his little daughter, Molly, while he was on the Island, but now the sense of her absence and the realisation that he would never see her again had come as a new shock. He couldn't shake off the sadness.

He took to walking out of the house every morning and wandering round the streets. He had no job, and did not know what he was going to do, and how he could reach out to his family again. Even Leah was growing impatient with him: 'We all still have to eat, William! The boys have done so much – you can't keep asking them to do your job!'

One day in March William walked into a nearby church. It was one he had never noticed before, not far from their home, called the Church of Christ Scientist. He didn't know what it meant, but the name rather appealed to him. He sat in one of the pews and after a while a man came up to him and asked if he could do anything for him. William shook his head, 'No – not unless you have any work for me. Or if you know a way to win back the trust of my sons ... who are all ashamed of me. I have recently returned from the Isle of Man, where I was interned as an enemy alien because I was born in Germany.'

'That must be very hard for them – and for you. Have you tried telling them what life was like for you there, in internment?'

'I am afraid I don't know how to talk to them at all any more. They have read and heard so many horror stories about German barbarity that they feel only shame about having a German father. I get angry with them sometimes – but I also want to weep for them.'

'I think you might begin by listening to their stories, and then by telling them yours. We must never lose our belief in one another's humanity, and telling our own story is often the best way.'

'Yes. Well, I might try. Thank you, Sir. And thank you for listening to me.'

'I am always here. I wish you and your family well.'

When William returned home that evening, he asked everyone to come into the sitting room, and began to describe to them what life on the Island had been like. At first his sons just stared at him, but after a while they began to rather enjoy his stories, especially when he told them about *'Schiebung'*. This was a running battle of wits between the prisoners and the guards. Prisoners sent out on work parties to neighbouring farms ran a black market in 'luxuries' – items such as newspapers, paper and crayons for drawing, apples and blackberries, farm implements for digging small garden plots where prisoners planted potatoes and turnips, that somehow appeared from nowhere. Alcohol was forbidden, so the discovery by the guards of empty wine and beer bottles hidden in odd corners was a complete mystery. This was all *'Schiebung'*.

'There was one especially clever one,' he told them. 'A church service ... no, listen, boys ... was only permitted once a month and had to be read out from a book, with no personal prayers and no sermon. One of our pastors, Pastor David, kept begging the guards to be allowed to deliver a short sermon "just to encourage the men to conform to camp rules."

Eventually they gave him permission, but only if he delivered it in the presence of a German-speaking guard. Pastor David arrived with his sermon all written out, and was told to hand it over to the waiting guard. At the end of the service the guard complained that he had not kept to the words of his script. "How could I?" he replied, "you were holding my paper!"'

William was delighted when Clifford and Leo both immediately shouted, '*Schiebung!*' and a second later all the others caught on and shouted it too, and everybody laughed.

✤

In May, William found part-time work as an assistant in a Manchester bookshop he had known in his days as a sales rep before the war. The manager was Tommy Rea, the son of Otto's friend Harry. Tommy had been shocked when he had bumped into William one day, walking round the streets of Manchester looking gaunt and miserable. Tommy was ten years older than William, but through their fathers' friendship they had known one another for years. When William told him he was still looking for work, Tommy said he'd be only too glad to have someone with William's experience to help in the shop, and soon realised that William, once so cheerful and easy-going, was now in a dangerously low state of mind.

Gerard Belringer advised William to come over to Liverpool and see Otto's friend, Sir Ronald Golding, to ask if he could help him get his old sales representative job back. In July an appointment was made for him to see Sir Ronald in his office. Sir Ronald told William that his own publishing venture had now been absorbed by a much bigger London publishing company, but in view of his long friendship with William's father, and William's own good record from when he had been working for him, he promised that he would recommend him to the Director of Marketing of the new Manchester office for Chapman and Hall, who coincidentally were the publishers of William's favourite author, Charles Dickens. Afterwards William went round to Gerard and Alice's home and told them how it had gone.

'Oh well done, Will! I'm sure this means you will get your old job back.' Alice said enthusiastically, kissing him. Gerard said, 'You may find Chapman and Hall will be concerned about taking on a sales representative with a German-sounding name.' He glanced at Alice, 'We all know how much damage any connection with Germany can cause. You and Leah really should think about formally changing the family name to something more English sounding. It could make a difference.'

Alice agreed. 'Emily and Freddie have already made arrangements to change their surnames to Logan, and Gerard and I have been trying to persuade Mama and Papa to do the same but, not surprisingly, Mama absolutely refuses even to consider it, and Papa says he is too old to worry about such things.'

William said, 'I will certainly think about it. But I want to wait a little longer before I even apply for the job. I need to be at home with Leah and the boys and not have to keep going away, at least until we know when this bloody war will end.... If it ever does,' he added gloomily.

'Not long now,' Gerard said confidently. William looked at him questioningly, but he just smiled. 'Truly, William. Not long now. Now the Americans are here.

*

Liverpool – 11 November 1918

Germany Signed Armistice

Our Terms Are Signed - The Great News – PEACE

Hostilities ceased on all fronts at eleven o'clock this morning.

The Terms:

> **Rhine Crossings to be occupied, including**
>> **Mainz, Goblentz and Cologne.**
>
> **Evacuate Alsace-Lorraine, Luxembourg**
>> **and Belgium.**
>
> **Surrender all U-Boats**
>
> **Treaties of Brest-Litovsk and Bucharest**
>> **wiped out.**
>
> **Disarming of huge part of the Fleet**
>
> **Allies right to occupy Heliogoland**
>
> **Surrender of 5,999 Locomotives and**
>> **150,000 wagons and 5000 Motor Lorries**
>
> **Give up 2,000 Aeroplanes**
>
> **To Pay Full Compensation**
>
> **Naval Air Forces to Disband**
>
> **Allies to Occupy Baltic and Kattegat Forts**
>
> **Return Russia's Warships**
>
> **ALL PRISONERS TO BE FREE**

Liverpool Echo, Monday 11 November 1918

Manchester – December 1918

Just before Christmas, Tommy showed William an American book that had come in to the shop that he said had caused a stir in America and now seemed to be becoming a big talking point in England.

'As a good old Catholic, it's not something I could take too seriously myself, Will, you know – some sort of mind-over-matter business I suppose you would call it – but people seem to think there might be something in it. I'd be glad of your own opinion as I know you are a great one for the deep thinking.'

The book was *Science and Health* by Mary Baker Eddy, who was described as the founder of the 'Church of Christ Scientist'. William took a copy of the book home. He remembered the church he had been into near his home when he had been at his lowest ebb, and the kind man there who had helped him begin to find a way to reach out to his family. He had never told Leah about this experience. He now realised that this book was written by the founder of the same branch of Christianity.

William was impressed by the book. He began to underline sentences. '*Love never loses sight of loveliness.... Men and women ought to ripen into health and immortality, instead of lapsing into darkness or gloom.... Immortal Mind feeds the body with supernal freshness and fairness, supplying it with beautiful images of thought ...*'

The author seemed to be saying that a truly spiritual mind could heal human suffering and disease through faith, which was better than any medicine or any doctor could do. Although William and his brother and sisters had all been brought up to admire the character of Jesus the good carpenter, and the family went to church together every Sunday, they had never discussed spiritual ideas at home. The church was something William had always enjoyed for the singing, but he usually paid little attention to the preaching. Leah always seemed to him to be far more devout. He thought of her almost as a saint, with her love and patience with him and all their children. Now he thought about the way that she had saved Sam from dying of diphtheria almost through sheer force of her love and will. And he remembered with anger how the doctors at the sanatorium had let his poor little Molly die.

He showed Leah some of the passages in the book and she read them carefully then looked up at him, puzzled.

'I think it is about something you already know, deep down, Leah. I think it is about the kind of person you already are, and we all need to become. Many of the things in this book seem to me to have been proved true in the camp. The men who kept hope in their hearts, and continued to live positive, good lives, all survived much better than the ones who let anger or fear or despair take hold of them.'

*

Liverpool – Christmas 1918

Otto asked all the family to come together at their home in Liverpool that Christmas. William had to work in the bookshop in the morning and would come down on the afternoon train, while Leah and all their sons travelled down in the morning; the four older boys would be staying the night with Gerard and Alice, while William, Leah and the three youngest were to stay with Otto and Anna. They had all gathered at Otto and Anna's house by mid-day, and the children were told that nobody was to be allowed into the music room except their uncle Freddie and auntie Emily.

A few snowflakes began to fall; Otto took all the boys and ten-year-old Maisie out into the garden, encouraging them to see if they could gather enough snow together to make a small snowman. The children kept running back into the house to warm their hands in the kitchen, making Anna exclaim as her floor grew wet with melting snow.

After a late lunch of soup and bread Anna insisted that all the children should go and lie down, dividing themselves between the four bedrooms. Otto went into the sitting room for his afternoon rest and Gerard left, saying he had some errands to run in town and would be back with Aunt Clara in time for the evening Christmas feast. A long Christmas letter from

Trude and Tom Metcalfe arrived, greeting them all but explaining that the journey from Scotland was too far for them to undertake in winter.

Anna, Alice and Emily were hard at work in the kitchen. Gerard and Alice had provided an enormous goose, so big it had made Anna scream when they first came into the kitchen bearing it. She had spent the morning making stock from the giblets and rubbing the bird all over with salt. Now she prepared a stuffing of apples, onions and herbs from the garden before somehow managing to squeeze the huge bird into the range. Emily was in charge of peeling the potatoes and parsnips, preparing them for roasting, while Alice made a big bowl of apple sauce and began to steam two large Christmas puddings she had made at home that autumn.

Later in the afternoon Freddie went to put the finishes touches to the secrets of the Music Room and Anna and Emily looked up in surprise when they heard a sudden loud crash and smothered laughter coming from there, just as Otto came through to the kitchen rubbing his eyes and asking what was going on. Nobody could tell him. There was silence, and then what sounded like a motor lorry driving away down the road. They all looked at one another, puzzled, but the disturbance was quickly forgotten because just at that moment William arrived from the station, and Gerard came into the kitchen with

Aunt Clara, who greeted them all with cries of welcome. She kissed Anna and hugged Otto and William and said, 'Now where are all those children I've come to see?'

At last everything was prepared and the children were summoned downstairs, Clara insisting that Sam and Freddy came down in their pyjamas, and everyone gathered in the dining room to enjoy their first family Christmas dinner together since 1914. To seat so many of them they had first had to clear the dining room of all furniture except for the table. Even the long table wasn't quite big enough for them all to have places, so Albert and Edgar had helped Freddie bring down two smaller ones from upstairs to extend its length.

Clara and Anna had worked all autumn embroidering a long white table cloth with patterns of golden-tipped leaves of holly and ivy. Now tall candles were lit all down its length, so when everyone sat down and began talking, Otto, sitting at the head of the table, could see their faces glowing in the warm flickering light.

Gerard was the last to appear, coming in from the garden with two magnums of champagne he had been hiding in the shed. Ignoring warning signals from Clara, Anna and Leah, he went round the table pouring some into everybody's glass – even Sam and Freddy's little cups. Then he held up his own glass and said, 'Tonight is important for every single member of our family – no-one must be left out of this toast. This is a Christmas night we hardly dared to dream could happen. Please will everyone raise their glass – or cup – with me and drink a toast to welcome home those two greatly admired and greatly loved men: Otto and William!'

'Otto and William!'

The two younger children giggled as they copied the grown-ups and sipped their champagne, clinking their mugs together for 'Grandpa and Papa!'

Then Otto stood up. 'Thank you, Gerard. I think we all know who should be celebrated this Christmas – our brave wives, and our wonderful sons and daughters and daughter-in-law, and of course, you Gerard, without whose help I doubt we have got home in time for this splendid Christmas feast. And all our wonderful grandchildren, who have had to spend their childhood growing up too fast. I am lost in admiration for the grace and courage and fortitude with which you have all en-dured these last years. Christmas Eve is a night that celebrates a holy family, and I would like you all to stand up now and raise your glasses with me: we celebrate the Holy Family – and our own family.'

'The Holy Family – and our own family!'

Anna got slowly to her feet. 'I would like to ask you all to do one more thing. I want you to thank God for the end of this terrible war and please will you all pray that Germany and England never fight each other ever again. Never! Never! Never again! I raise my own glass in a prayer for everlasting peace and friendship.'

'Everlasting peace and friendship.'

Otto sat quietly at the head of the table, watching as everyone chattered and laughed and told stories, almost as though there had been no four-year gap since the last time they had celebrated Christmas night together. He smiled at Anna, who was listening to William and Gerard sitting on either side of her, discussing some new book William was excited about and wanted his mother and sister and Gerard to read. He heard Gerard say, 'It is interesting. I remember it was all the rage in America some time ago. But it's not really my sort of thing, I'm afraid.' Anna exclaimed in her old excitable way, 'Oh! Such a cynic, Gerard! I shall read it, Wilhelm!'

She was still pale and he saw she was hardly eating anything but Otto was happy that at least she seemed to be recovering some of her old sparkle. He suddenly felt overwhelmed by something that felt even deeper than happiness and struggled to hold back his tears.

The children were all getting merry on the tiny bit of champagne they had drunk, and Otto smiled as Clara wagged her finger at them and Leah tried to keep them in order, with little success. Philip and Clifford were making up silly new words for Christmas carols and ordering Sam and Freddy to sing them, while Albert and Edgar tried to make grown up conversation with Maisie, who was laughing at them. Their Uncle Freddie wheeled in the giant roasted goose and Otto asked Gerard to carve, while Leo, Alice and Emily handed round roast potatoes and honey-covered parsnips.

Later, everyone gasped and cheered when Alice and Emily came in, each bearing a large Christmas pudding decorated with holly and alight with wild blue flames. Leah and William sang '*In dulci jubilo*' while the pudding was being served. Then Otto told everyone they must make their new year wish before they ate.

As the table was being cleared, Otto went to look out of the window and then quickly drew back the curtains. Everyone cheered again when they saw thousands of snowflakes shining in the darkness and settling in the garden. 'That was my wish!' Sam squeaked. 'And mine!' said Freddy. 'And mine,' said Otto. Before anyone could stop them all the children shouted and jumped down from the table to put on their wellingtons and coats and run out into the snow storm.

Leah, William, Emily, Gerard and Alice helped clear everything away into the kitchen and began to wash up while Otto
and Anna sat by the fire in the sitting room with Clara, who
had made Sam and little Freddy come in from the garden to sit
with them. Soon she began telling them it was time for bed, but
Anna said, 'they must just see the music room first, Clara. I
believe Freddie and Emily have prepared a surprise for us all.'

Freddie was at that moment supervising the older children,
who were having noisy snowball fights in the garden. When
the clock chimed half past eleven Otto stood up and said, 'I
think it is time,' and went and summoned everyone indoors to
take off wet clothes and boots. Emily and Freddie disappeared
into the music room, shutting the door behind them. After five
minutes they opened the door and said, 'You can all come in
now.'

In the middle of the room sat a tall fir tree that reached the
ceiling, decorated with dozens of tiny silver paper bells and
stars. There were forty little burning candles fastened to the
tree – the only light in the room. The children, having been
vigorously rubbed dry by Clara, came running in and then
stood quite shyly in front of the scene that met them.

The room seemed like a magic cavern, its walls hung with
winter greenery. At the foot of the tree stood a crib scene that
Anna had had as a child, and her sister, Liese, had brought over

for her when she had come to visit them ten years earlier. In the little wooden stable stood the familiar slightly lopsided manger with a sleeping baby watched over by the two painted wooden figures of Mary and Joseph. There was a donkey, a shepherd and a small lamb. In the flickering candle-light from the tree, the scene came magically alive.

As they all stood quietly taking in the scene, Otto noticed something half-hidden in the dark corner of the room behind the tree. Sitting under a pile of wrapped parcels he could just make out a strangely familiar shape. He had to hold on to Anna for a moment, and then he pointed it out to her. It took her a moment to see what he was looking at and then she gave a little scream.

Otto turned round to see Emily and Freddie both beaming with excitement, while Gerard and Alice were watching him anxiously. Gerard began to say, 'Otto, we are only sorry it couldn't be ...' but before he could finish Otto had come over and seized them in great bear hugs. He couldn't speak. Anna kept saying, 'But how? How can it...? Where...? Where did it come from?'

Freddie laughed happily and said, 'Didn't you hear the crash it made coming in through the window? We were afraid you would all come running.'

'Oh! Oh! Yes! But we had no idea....'

'Gerard went to collect it when he went for Aunt Clara, and the delivery lorry followed him round to the back of the house so that they could lift it in through the music room window. There were four men manhandling the thing from outside the window but it landed with such a crash on my side because I couldn't steady it – we were sure you must have heard!'

Otto was still speechless. Gerard said, 'It was all Freddie's idea, Otto. He and Emily both wanted so much to do it. I only helped a little, and I am only sorry we couldn't run to at least a baby grand piano ...'

Freddie was interrupting, 'No, no – we owe it all to Gerard ...'

Otto said, 'Oh Gerard, Freddie, dearest Emily ... I cannot find the words to tell you what joy this has brought me – and surprise! I never thought ...' He turned to put his arm around Anna. 'We shall have music in this house again, Anna! Oh Gerard, and all of you – how can we ever thank you enough for this precious gift?'

William was looking at his brother and sisters a little sadly, 'I am a little upset that we knew nothing about this. You know that Leah and I and the boys would have all wanted to share in the gift.'

Gerard said quickly, 'We knew you would, Wills. But you know how much joy you and Leah have already given Otto and

Anna with your wonderful family of boys. We thought that such a big present was one that none of us could match. So we hoped you would allow us the privilege of being the ones to give them this.'

William smiled ruefully and shook his head, then went and hugged his father and mother and Anna said, 'Oh Wilhelm, the love and happiness you and your family have given us can never be measured.'

Clara said firmly – 'We must put these little ones to bed now, Leah.' Everyone looked at her in surprise. Clara put her fingers to her lips and led Anna and Leah through to the sitting room where they found Sam and Freddy curled up fast asleep on the settee. Leah smiled lovingly at them but she said, 'Like two little cats. Of course, Clara. But please wait one little minute more – for our old family tradition.' She picked up Sam, and Clara picked up Freddy and they went back to the music room. Otto had gone cautiously round behind the tree and lifted the lid of the Broadwood piano. He played one note and then he looked round through the candle-lit branches at his family. Anna started to sing.

'Stille nacht! Heilige nacht!'
They all joined in.
'Alles schlaft; einsam wacht

Nur das traute heilege Paar,

Holder Knab im lockigten Haar,

Schlafe in himmlishcher Ruh!

Schlafe in himmlischer Ruh!'

Then Clara said, 'But now it is long past time for these little ones to *schlafe in himmlischer Ruh!* Let me take them up to bed please, Leah? I'd love to tuck them in.'

12

The Aftermath

Manchester – January 1919

When William and Leah finally completed the formalities early in January, the family name was officially changed to Logan. William, however, still did not apply for British citizenship.

He had begun reading out loud to the family from the book of *Science and Health* which had so caught his own attention and admiration. He took Leah along to meet the man, Richard Holding, in the nearby Church of Christ Scientist who had encouraged him when he had been in the depths of despair about ever winning back his sons' love and respect.

William took the whole family along to see Richard at one of their meetings, and then enrolled them all into the Sunday school so that they could learn about it together. He told them, 'I want all of you to become broadminded, broad-shouldered, broad-hearted men. You have all had to face a lot of hardship and had many disappointments in your young lives, but now we can all learn to have a positive attitude and the expectation of good winning over evil. There is infinite goodness in the world which we can all have confidence in. If we firmly believe in the power of this goodness, all will be well.'

*

Liverpool – January 1919

Towards the end of January Otto realised that Anna was losing her strength. After the supreme effort she had made over Christmas, and ever since William and his family had left to return to Manchester the following day, she had been growing much quieter. For the first time since he had known her she wanted to sleep late in the mornings, and then would sometimes fall asleep again in the middle of the afternoon. Emily was on holiday from school and still living at home, so she was preparing their meals and looking after the house.

Although she had had many admirers as she grew into a young woman, including her cousin Hans, Emily had only experienced one serious love affair. Her tutor at her teacher training college, Giles Carter, was tall and solemn and gangly; he was clever and a wonderfully inspiring teacher – above all, he made her laugh. When his own admiration of her had become clear, she had come to love him, and the outbreak of war had increased the intensity of both their feelings. They became lovers; then Giles proposed to her and she had accepted him.

They decided to keep their engagement secret in the hope that the war would soon be over, and any awkwardness about her parents' nationality could be avoided. After the sinking of the *Lusitania* in 1915, however, although he was in a reserved occupation, along with many young men in Liverpool, Giles had joined up.

Freddie, who had already guessed her secret, was the only one Emily could talk to about him – Anna was preoccupied with her terror and anxiety about Otto and William. When Giles' father wrote to Emily in 1916 that they had received a telegram saying that Giles had been killed in action on 1 July, Emily told only Freddie.

After the declaration of peace, Giles' father sent Emily the Military Cross Giles had been awarded after the battle of the Somme, with a kind letter:

'His mother and I were reluctant at first to part with this. He was our only son. But I know you were our son's one true love, and he would want you to have this to keep, along with your memory of him.'

Emily kept the letter together with Giles' medal, hidden in a box.

*

Liverpool – April 1919

Otto and Freddie moved the sitting room settee into the music room so that Anna could be comfortable there while he played for her after supper, but instead of sewing or singing or turning the pages for him, as she would have done in the past, now she lay down and invariably fell asleep. One evening she asked him to make her a cup of chocolate before she went up to bed. He went out to ask Emily to make it, and waited in the kitchen talking to her while the milk was warming. They went back together to Anna in the music room where, as soon as he saw her, Otto knew that Anna was not asleep. She had slipped quietly away from him.

Two weeks later, there was an outbreak of the Asian 'flu epidemic that had been devastating Europe and America for nearly a year. Alice fell ill. Gerard found a young nurse to come and live in the house with them to look after her night and day. Emily went over to their house each day to spend time with Maisie while her mother was too ill to look after her. Alice at thirty-four years old was still young and strong, but in May, just over a month after they had buried Anna, she too passed away. Gerard arranged for her to be buried in Anfield cemetery beside her mother.

Gerard went abroad the day after Alice's funeral, and Emily moved into his house to look after their distraught daughter, Maisie. They didn't know how long Gerard was going to be away.

*

Manchester – June 1919

Shortly after his forty-fifth birthday, William put in his application for a job in the office of Chapman and Hall. He had a good
reference from Sir Ronald and in June he was offered a one-
year contract to work in their northern publicity department,
not as a travelling sales rep but in the office, writing advertis-
ing copy and jacket copy for all the 'northern' books on the
authors' list they had acquired from Sir Ronald's old company.
William went round to the bookshop to break the news to
Tommy, and to thank him for all the help he had given him
through his dark days. Tommy shook him warmly by the hand:
'Good man yourself, Will! And you know there will always be
a warm welcome for you back here any day you want.'

*

Liverpool – August 1919

Gerard stayed away for three months, only contacting Maisie
and Emily occasionally by letter. When he eventually returned
to Liverpool, he asked Emily if she would keep coming over to
be a companion for Maisie during the school holidays.

Like many young women of her generation, with so many
young men killed and having lost Giles, Emily assumed that
she would never marry. When, six months after Alice's death,
Gerard proposed to her, telling her honestly that his reason was
that he wanted Maisie to have the stability of someone she

knew and loved as a permanent part of her life, Emily accepted.

'You mustn't hope for too much from me, Emily. Having you to live here with us has been wonderful for Maisie and I am enormously grateful. I have always loved you like a young sister but I don't think I can be much of a husband for you. I am far too old for you, for one thing.'

Emily smiled at him and said, 'I think we will manage very well, my dear brother Gerard!'

When they told Otto, he was surprised, but he shook Gerard warmly by the hand and said he was very happy for them both. He had been privately worrying about how quiet Emily had seemed ever since his return from Knockaloe. He hoped this would give her a happier life.

Freddie had looked shocked when she told him, and then he said doubtfully, 'I suppose you know what you are doing, Em. But are you sure this is a good idea?'

'Maisie needs me.'

'Yes, but does he need you? You can help Maisie without sacrificing yourself. Are you really sure he can make you happy? You're the only one whose happiness matters to me.'

'I know. I know. Dear Freddie, what would I do without you? But please don't worry. I believe in his own way he does need me and he will come to love me in time. You know I have always …'

'Of course I know. That's what worries me.'

Gerard was often away for weeks at a time, often without telling her where he was going or for how long, but Emily was more or less contented with her life. She was grieving for her mother and sister as well as Giles, and was relieved to be able to live quietly alone in the house with Maisie. There were no servants now – they had all left in 1915 – but Emily preferred to be kept busy now that she was no longer teaching.

As well as Maisie, Freddie and Otto still needed her too. She went to see them every day when Maisie was at school, and during the holidays they would both go over together. Otto helped Maisie with her piano lessons, and Emily and Freddie gave her cookery lessons.

Emily also began to take Maisie over to Manchester for long visits during the school holidays, so that she could spend time with her cousins. The boys all spoiled her and competed for her admiration and attention. William, too, always made a big fuss of the little girl whenever she came to stay with them, and would write her weekly letters when she returned home to Liverpool.

*

Liverpool – January 1923

In January Otto died, a tired old man, and was buried beside Anna and Alice in Anfield cemetery.

Once again William, Freddie and Gerard were standing by the family graveside, this time all William's sons were there too, even the youngest two. Sir Ronald Golding and Otto's old friend Harry Rea with his son, Tommy, stood with them. As the family remained silent, Harry said, 'I would like to say a few words about this fine man, if I may?' William looked at him gratefully, and Gerard and Sir Ronald nodded in sympathetic agreement.

'My friend, Otto Lohmann, was a great man, a free citizen who brought his own greatest gifts to this city of ours   the gift of music and the gift of the love of music. He taught so many of us not only how to play, but the far greater gift of how to listen to music. The way he and his family, especially his dear wife Anna, have been treated over these past few years is beyond our understanding. But I believe that he and Anna and their beloved daughter, Alice, are together now, and have all been welcomed in a far better place as free citizens of the kingdom of God.'

13

Moving On

Liverpool – February 1923

One week after Otto's funeral, Freddie disappeared without saying a word to anyone. For the next twenty years nobody in the family heard from him or knew where or why he had gone. Only Emily had been left a short note,

'Dear Emily, I can't stay here any longer. I know you will understand. I will miss you. I need to find my own way. I promise you I will come back to see you one day. Be happy, please. Your affectionate brother, Freddie.'

*

Immediately after the war, Gerard Belringer's fortunes were far more reduced than he had let anyone realise. Scandal had attached to his name after the sinking of the *Lusitania* by a German ship that his company had supplied parts for, and he had been obliged to sell all his interest in the shipping company that had always been his main source of income. Even in his days of prosperity he had borrowed extensively to support his extravagant lifestyle, and the money from the enforced sale of the company had largely gone on repaying loans that were all immediately called in by his bank and creditors. Even Emily remained in the dark about the real state of his affairs. She realised he was no longer the wealthy man he had once been, but since he had been exonerated from all blame, she supposed he would recover quickly and return to his old way of life.

Emily would sometimes go into his study to take him a cup of coffee and find Gerard sitting at his desk, his head down, deep in thought, frowning and tapping one hand rapidly with a half pencil. She had once found a little pile of these pencils on his desk, all carefully sliced down the middle and with the lead removed and had nearly thrown them away. When she asked him about them he had laughed, 'Oh they are my tappers. I need to tap in order to think. They were Alice's idea.'

Outwardly he did indeed carry on in much the same way as before. He was always looking for new opportunities to make money and to maintain his reputation for being a man to watch. He continued to entertain his old contacts to expensive lunches and to be seen at all the important civic events. His loud laugh, enthusiastic conversation and expensive clothes made him stand out in public places, but now there was no expense account to draw on. He was borrowing heavily once again, and he had only a limited time to re-establish himself before even his very patient and understanding bank manager stopped the vital money supply again.

He sold his yacht, which was bought by a wealthy American who had come to Britain to explore the possibilities of making a film about the sinking of the *Lusitania*. He had been curious to learn about Gerard's part in the story, and when the two men had met, the American was charmed by Gerard. Gerard himself had quickly realised that this film could be an ideal opportunity for his own part in the drama to be shown in a highly favourable and rather intriguing light. It was an image that appealed to him. He worked hard to find British backers and expert advisers for the enterprise.

The American lived aboard the yacht whenever he was over in Liverpool, but as that was for only two months a year, Gerard persuaded him that it would add to his project's prestige if he, Gerard, were to continue to have use of the yacht for two or three weekends a year for his famous champagne lunches, where politicians, civic leaders and businessmen met privately, and where potential backers for the film project might now be casually introduced to the idea

Giles Carter had left Emily with his own Crystal radio set when he had departed for France in 1915. She had never used it, but when Gerard left for a three month trip to America, she found it again, and got it out. Maisie had great fun trying to tune into the crackly sounding programmes.

Gerard came home unexpectedly early one evening, and found Emily and Maisie dancing round the room to orchestra music coming from the radio. He had come quietly into the room without them realising and stood watching them for some moments before suddenly dancing into the room to join them, twirling Maisie round and making her scream with laughter and surprise. Then he had taken Emily in his arms and danced with her. That night Gerard had come into Emily's room for the first time since they were married.

The next day he was cheerful and excited. At breakfast he said to them both, 'Seeing you dancing last night has given me the most wonderful idea. Radio. That's how we're going to restore the family fortunes!'

Emily laughed, 'Whatever do you mean?'

'In America radio is huge, my dears. I just foolishly hadn't realised how much people here would be listening to it too – and in their homes – like you two last night. That old machine of yours is nearly defunct – I shall buy a new one. I've been so stupid not to think of it before. Come with me, Maisie No time to lose!'

He jumped up, picked Maisie up out of her chair and waltzed her round the room and out of the door. Emily was left sitting alone at the breakfast table. She heard them go out through the front door. A moment later, Gerard came back in,

'Just taking Maisie into town for the day. We'll be back with you tonight! With a new radio!' He kissed her quickly on the cheek, and was gone.

*

Manchester – June 1923

Even after they were both married, Albert and Edgar continued to contribute part of their earnings to Leah. The four younger children were all still at school, and even though he now had a permanent, post with Chapman and Hall, William's salary was still barely enough to support them all.

Edgar was now working as a qualified engineer, and Albert was being sent to Nigeria by his firm for two years to help train young apprentices in the company's Lagos factory. While he was away, William wrote to him every week, his letters always full of Christian Science precepts: *Be quiet when you have nothing to say – do not be afraid of any feeling of lack. What is the trend of to-day? It is hurry, bustle, scurry. Few people leave themselves time to think....'*

In 1925 Albert returned from Africa and he and Edgar went together to see Gerard for advice about setting up a small business. Gerard suggested that they should think about the growing number of people now acquiring private cars. He told them: 'A small business that could supply spare parts and do repairs might do very well in the future.' The boys were enthusiastic, and Gerard offered to invest some of his own money in the enterprise to get them started. He also recommended that they employ his old chauffeur as an experienced motor technician.

Leo had left school at fourteen in order to help his mother during the last year of the war, but soon after William came home, Leo's headmaster had recognised him one day working in the bookshop and had persuaded him to let Leo go back for another year to take his higher school certificate. During his final term Leo had won a scholarship to study art in Italy. He ran straight home to tell Leah, dancing with excitement. When William came home that evening they told him the great news together.

William shook Leo's hand. 'That is a truly wonderful achievement, son. I know you will be a great artist one day. But I hope you understand that your mother needs you here now, don't you?'

'Oh!' Leo experienced a shock of understanding.

'It would cost a great deal of money, Leo. Times are hard. But you can still feel very proud of yourself. You have had a great achievement – no-one can take that away from you.'

'But ... do you mean ... you think I must not go to Italy?'

'Do *you* think you should go?'

'But I've won....' Leo looked at his mother. She wasn't looking at him. She was looking at William with a strange expression.

Then she said, 'Leo, you are such a wonderful elder brother to the younger boys. You are teaching them so much about art and they would miss you terribly ... we all would.'

Leo said sadly, 'So I suppose - I shouldn't go.'

William shook Leo's hand again. 'I am very proud of you, son. And you can feel very proud of yourself.'

Leo left school at the end of term and found work as a draftsman in the publicity department of a big local company. It allowed him to develop his drawing skill, and he amused himself at home passing on all he knew about colour and perspective to Sam and Fred, who were both enthusiastic and diligent pupils. Leo still secretly dreamed of becoming an architect one day.

Over the next ten years, as Gerard had predicted, Albert and Edgar's partnership in the motor trade gradually began to do well. Philip, a year younger than Leo, had gone to work with Albert and Edgar as an apprentice as soon as he left school.

There was growing demand for privately owned cars, which were now being designed for recreation and sport as well as business, and more and more people needed the services of experienced mechanics to keep them on the road.

Edgar, temperamentally the more ambitious of the two brothers, was always eager to expand and invest in new ideas and equipment, while Albert, with a nature more like their father's, enjoyed talking to the customers and teaching them about what their new cars could do. He was happy to let Edgar make the major management decisions.

Albert's lively young wife, Isobel, however, thought that he was allowing Edgar to have far too much control over how the business was run. She kept urging Albert to be more decisive, but Albert had never been as interested in the business side of the motor trade as his brother, and Edgar soon grew irritated by any interference or suggestions Albert, urged on by Isobel, tried to make. The brothers quarrelled and in spite of all William's attempts to act as peace-maker, working together became unpleasant.

'I don't think Isobel should be interfering in Albert's business, Will,' Leah told her husband. She had been suspicious of Albert's pushy young bride from the start, and now she wanted to put her in her place. William had laughed. 'But Isobel is wonderful! And our Albert needs her in the same way that I need you, Leah! We both need our bossy wives to keep us in order!'

'Me? Bossy? William! How can you?' Leah looked hurt. He laughed again and hugged her. 'I think we must give Isobel a chance, my dear. She is a good influence on him, and she is making Albert happy.'

Isobel's next suggestion was that Albert should ask Edgar to buy him out, and invest the money in a business that they could run together. At first Edgar refused outright, not wanting to release any capital at this early stage of the still embryonic company, and was persuaded only when Gerard Belringer stepped in and offered to invest more money in the business, in return for his appointment as executive Chairman.

Albert and Isobel found a small shop for sale close to a railway station in a town outside Manchester and went ahead with converting it into a café. Many people were choosing to move out of the city centre and their business became a flourishing concern, serving breakfast to the growing number of commuters who passed through the station every day. Under Isobel's tuition, Albert found he had a talent for cooking simple dishes as well as charming the customers; once again he was content to let his business partner – this time his wife, Isobel – take charge of the management.

Clifford still had another two years to go at school and his teachers thought he could do well in his school certificate exams providing he worked hard. Clifford always took a holiday job in a local store, helping in the shop and delivering groceries to customers. He started supplying William with plants and seeds on a regular basis so that William could grow more vegetables in his garden. Like Otto before him, William had discovered the joy of gardening, and as well as rows of potatoes and beans, he had planted a small orchard of apple and pear trees, where Leah's hens could scratch about. Gardening for healthy food tied in with his new deeply held Christian Science beliefs, with which he had also tried to imbue all his sons. He and Leah still sometimes sang in the parish church choir, but they always went to meetings in the Reading Room, along with Albert and Eddie and their wives; the younger boys all attended the Christian Science Sunday school.

Clifford's elder brothers suspected he was back to his old tricks of pilfering. It had been forgivable during the war, when they had all taken their turn at scavenging from the local fields, but they were pretty sure that Clifford was now taking things from the store where he worked. Leo suspected that as well as bringing garden plants home for William, Clifford was making more serious money selling stolen goods to his friends.

Leah was upset and angry with Leo when he reported his suspicions to her. 'No son of mine would do anything dishonest! How could you even think such a thing, Leo?'

When William came home from work that night, she told him what Leo had said. 'I'm sure it's not true, Will. But what should we do?'

'I will have a word with Clifford, Leah. I am certain he would never seriously steal anything – but he's young and perhaps he doesn't understand. We don't want him getting into any trouble.'

When the boys were in bed, William went up to the room Clifford shared with Leo and Philip. His brothers were both sitting up in bed reading, but Clifford was sound asleep. William sat on his son's bed and shook him awake. He sat up and looked blearily at his father. 'Your mother and I are worried, Clifford. What is all this I hear that you have been stealing things from your employer?'

Clifford rubbed his eyes. 'What?'

'Have you been stealing from the shop where you work?'

Clifford looked at Leo and Philip, who were both now watching him gravely, and then back at his father's serious face. He slowly broke into a grin: *'Schiebung!'*

'Clifford!' Leo and William both shouted together. William was looking appalled.

Clifford said earnestly, 'Father, I promise you – I have only ever taken things that they don't want any more.'

'Whatever can you mean, Clifford?'

'Oh, you know. There are so many things that have grown old and musty sitting on the back of the shelves. Nobody will buy them. They just take up room. I'm actually *helping* the manager by making more space for things he *can* sell. I'm doing him a good turn. It's just that he doesn't really know about it....'

'Oh Clifford, you are still very young. Your mother and I are worried that you are turning down a wrong path at the moment, but it is not too late. I do assure you that you will only have a good, happy life if you have an honest one. There is no other way, Clifford.'

'Yes, Father. But I don't think there is anything *really* dishonest in what I did ... I'm not taking anything that anybody wants....' He stopped when he saw his father's expression. 'But I won't do anything that worries you and Mother, I promise.'

'Well please make sure you keep your promise, Clifford.'

William stood up and went to the door. 'Turn your light out soon please, Leo. Don't read too late. You all need your sleep.'

When he had shut their door he could hear Clifford and Leo arguing in loud whispers. He quickly opened it again and they both fell silent.

'All go to sleep now. Good night, boys.'

'Good night, Father.'

The two youngest boys, Sam and Freddy, were both very attached to their mother. Freddy especially loved singing with her in his beautiful, clear treble. Leah had taught them both some of the songs she used to perform in her Mossley Hill Choir days so that they could all sing them together.

Sam, too, during his long, slow period of recovery from diphtheria had become closely bonded to Leah and always felt very protective of her. He used to say, 'I will look after you, Mother. When I am grown up I shall be a rich man and you will live in a big house and we shall all eat strawberries and chocolate and oranges every Christmas!'

Part of the younger boys' reluctance to accept William after his return from the Isle of Man had been because he seemed to be taking up so much of their mother's time – time that she had once spent with them. Leah was well aware of the problem, so she had encouraged William to tell his young sons bedtime stories every night when he got home from his work, so that they would begin to feel closer to him. One evening, when she was downstairs preparing his supper, she heard William's light baritone and two treble voices all singing together, and smiled with relief.

Sam was a serious boy. He was very skinny, and by the time he was eleven, he had grown nearly as tall as his mother. He had enormous feet, and Leah wondered whether he would grow to be a giant, like his cousin Hans. Encouraged by his teachers, Sam worked extremely hard at school, and when he was eleven, to his great surprise and delight, he was offered a place at Manchester Grammar. Sam believed he was now on his way to fulfilling his ambition to become a rich man.

At the end of the summer holidays, Leah showed him a letter from the local secondary school, where all the boys had gone and where Clifford was still a pupil, saying they were looking forward to welcoming him at the beginning of the following term. Sam stared at the letter, looking puzzled.

'But I'm not ... I'm going to Manchester Grammar, Mother! Don't you remember?'

'I'm sorry, Sam. They did send your father some paper he had to sign, agreeing that he would pay for you to go to the Grammar, but somehow ... I think he must have lost it. He has so much on his mind with his important new job and worrying about us all. And you know, Sam, it would have been very expensive for him. But never mind. You are such a clever boy, and you remember how much Leo enjoyed himself at this school, don't you? And look at what he has achieved! I know you will be a great success.'

Sam looked at his mother in shocked disbelief: 'He can't have lost it! It was so important! I will never ever forgive him for this!'

14

'On the Romp'

Leipzig – July 1931

In 1931 William was promoted to become the Northern Region Marketing Director for Chapman and Hall, and that summer he decided to accompany some of the senior editors of the parent company to the annual Leipzig Book Fair. He intended to visit his Aunt Liese and the family in Berlin as well as staying with his cousin Hans, who was now living and working as a professional architect in Leipzig. Hans, who had arrived back in Germany from America five years earlier, had sent William a postcard:

'Now I will show you Dresden! Our planned trip was rudely interrupted when we last met!'

Travelling across to Hamburg on the ferry, William tried to imagine the first crossing, when he had come as a baby with his parents and his aunts Clara and Trude. His mother and father had told him so often about that first journey and Otto's famous decision that they would all become 'citizens of the world'. Now Will walked all round the deck, leaning over the rails on either side of the boat and then at the back of the steamer, trying to visualise it all. Under a flight of steps leading up to the top deck, he found a long bench where he sat down and smoked a cigarette. He could hear sounds of loud laughter coming through the salon doors.

Clara had died earlier in the year aged sixty-seven, and William missed her. She had always been a great support to him and Leah, and he felt sad that she could not have found more happiness for herself. He didn't know if there was anyone left in Hamburg from his father's side of the family who might remember her as a child – he would have liked to have found someone in Germany to tell. 'But at least I can tell Hans. I am sure that he remembers her.'

In Leipzig, all the hotel rooms were taken by senior publishers from the major European houses, and the bars were full of loud masculine voices exchanging gossip. William had been invited to stay with Hans and his wife and was happy to keep out of everybody's way, although he would have to visit the Fair on Monday to justify his firm sending him over.

Hans Schindler and his American wife, Shirley, welcomed William warmly to their home in a large modern apartment overlooking White Elster River. William thought he had never met a couple where the man was as tall as Hans or the wife as short as Shirley. Hans hugged him. 'I'm so happy that you have "made it" over here at long last Will! I've told Shirley all about you and about our thwarted plans for your visit all those years ago!'

'I see you have managed to replace your "Liverpool" accent with an American one, Hans.'

'My mother even accuses me of speaking German with an American accent now. And we all know who is to blame for that!' He smiled at his tiny wife, and they all laughed.

'How do you do, Shirley? Wherever did you find this great giant?'

Shirley said, 'It was a shipboard romance, Will. I guess you are wondering how our eyes could ever have met. Me being so little and all?'

'Shirley might not have noticed me – but I for sure noticed her! We met on the boat bringing me home from the States. Shirley was with her parents on a trip to Europe. I just walked into the salon one morning and there she was – the most beautiful girl on the ship.' They smiled affectionately at one another. 'By far! So two months later we both went to wave her parents goodbye when they sailed back home to America. And then I spent the next six months showing Shirley all the places I had once been planning to show you, Will.'

'And I am very much looking forward to seeing some of them now that I am finally here – I am only sorry it has taken me so long!'

'Well as you are here for such a short while, there will only be time for us to show you around Leipzig itself and then perhaps pay a brief visit to Dresden, I think. But there is much for you to see and enjoy here. I will show you St Thomas Cathedral where Johann Sebastian Bach worked as a *Kapellmeister* and where he is buried. But you must promise us to come again for longer – and to bring the amazing Leah with you next time, Will.'

William looked serious. 'I do hope that we will both be able to come together one day, Hans. I'd like all our sons to come here too. It is just....' He shook his head doubtfully.

'The war has made everything very hard ... for us all. When you go to Berlin, I think you will be a little shocked.'

'They called us "enemy aliens" Hans! My wonderful father – you will remember how the city had been honouring him barely a year before! It has taken us all such a long time to get family life back to normal. The whole country is still having difficulty recovering after the loss of so many young men and so many hopes and dreams ... and there are so many badly wounded ex-servicemen all over the city these days who are having to beg for a living. For some of our fellow countrymen, it is understandable that we are still "enemy aliens". As you know, I've changed the family name – but not my own nationality. That would feel like a betrayal somehow.'

'It was a little different for me, because England was not my homeland. And there is much sadness and loss of life here too, Will. You will know that my brothers were both killed. And so many more. I only was lucky to escape it all, thanks to your Gerard Belringer.'

'We received your mother's sad letter about your brothers. And Hermann Von Treitsche – he too was killed?'

'I am sorry to say that the General shot himself. He couldn't accept the terms of the peace treaty. He left a note saying that his men had been betrayed by the politicians.'

'Very sad. We were just relieved it was all over at last.'

'Gerard wrote to us when your mother and sister died so soon afterwards, and now your wonderful father ... I was so sorry, Will. Your family were all very good to me. It was such a happy time until ...'

'Until all hell broke loose. Yes. It seems unreal now somehow. And dear Aunt Clara – do you remember her? She too has died recently.'

'I am very sorry – I remember she seemed a very kind lady. But the fair Emily is well?'

'Did you know she is married to Gerard now?

'Oh yes. Gerard has been to see us. And he told us about his daughter Maisie, who he says hopes to be a famous writer one day!'

'Yes, I have been encouraging her. We all love Maisie. She has come into our lives like an angel to stop us feeling so sad about losing our own beautiful daughter, Molly. And how is your mother, Hans? And your sisters – Margarethe and Eva?'

'My mother and sisters are all well, thank you. They are busy preparing an enormous feast for your day in Berlin! I think you are promised to go there to see them all on Tuesday?'

'Yes, then I need to take the train back to Hamburg on Wednesday to get the ferry home.'

'You will have a surprise when you see Margarethe, I think, Will.'

'A surprise?'

'I shall leave it as a surprise. But this only gives me a little time to show you the sights of Leipzig, Sunday to show you Dresden, and Monday I believe you wish to pretend to have some business in Leipzig?'

'Pretend! Show some respect! I will have you know I am very senior management these days, young Hans.'

'Oh of course you are, Will. How could I have forgotten you have reached such eminence?'

*

Berlin - Tuesday

On his arrival, William was greeted with warmth by his Aunt Liese.

'We are all so happy to see you, Wilhelm. And my wonderful Hans – did you find him well?'

'Very well. He and Shirley seem very happy. They showed me all the sights of Leipzig, and Hans and I had a great day out together in Dresden. What a beautiful city! I have never seen so much elegant architecture all in one place. And in Leipzig, Hans and Shirley have a beautiful home. Hans is having a great success in his work.'

'We are all so proud of him.'

William was dismayed when she suddenly burst into tears. 'I am so sorry, Wilhelm. But my poor sister! What she must have suffered! And your own sister, the beautiful Alice. So much sadness. So much sadness everywhere since I was last visiting you.'

'We have been living through some dark days, Aunt Liese. But I believe we must keep hopeful if we are to help build a better future for our children.'

'I am afraid there is not much hope to be found in Germany today, Wilhelm. I have never known such hard times. Everyone is struggling even to survive.'

'It is the same in England. We are all paying a heavy price for a war that has achieved nothing but misery for all of us....'

'Well, well – no politics today, Wilhelm! Now, I must warn you that Margarethe and Eva, my daughters, do not speak very good English. But we are all so happy to see you here at last. We have prepared a feast for you, just like my darling Anina, your mother, used to cook. We hope to make you feel at home with us.'

'I am so looking forward to meeting my cousins. I usually understand German, but I cannot speak it, I am afraid. Almost the only German I learnt was in the songs we sang. But my mother would sometimes talk to me secretly in German, especially if ever I was ill. So I am sure we will all manage to communicate somehow.'

'You will get quite a big surprise when you meet my sister Margarethe, I think.'

'Hans said the same thing! But he wouldn't tell me why.'

'Ah! Well it is because she looks so exactly like your dear mother.' Liese sighed heavily again.

'Well that will make me love her even more!'

'I hope so, Wilhelm. Eva and Hans take more after my husband's family. You didn't meet Herr Schindler when we visited England, I think?'

'No. I was living in Manchester when you came. I came over to see you and Hans in Liverpool, but Herr Schindler was still in London that day.'

'Well, you will meet him tonight.' She sighed: 'It is so sad that we have all had to grow so old before we could get to know each other well.'

'You are not so old, Aunt Liese!'

'Ah no! At least not too old to show you Berlin, and the house where your mother and I were born and we all grew up. You will see the old family silk and velvet factory – although I am afraid it is in sad decline these days. My husband and brother have closed it down and want to sell it – but who can afford to buy such a place these days?'

*

William's tour of Berlin was dutifully completed, but it had rather depressed him, and when he returned home he would talk only about Dresden. A week after his return home, his own postcard from there arrived:

3/9/31. On the romp in Dresden! Dresden is just about 3 times the size of M/e that is – old and new Dresden – two cities rolled into one.

Father

Postcard sent from Dresden by Will

*

Liverpool 1931

In spite of the Wall Street crash, Gerard had just managed to remain solvent. The *Lusitania* film project hadn't yet become a reality, but it had given him some invaluable American business contacts. His investment in Edgar's motor car business was still paying dividends. His own radio project had taken off, and now he not only owned a profitable company that designed and built new radio systems, he had also been taken on as an unofficial adviser to John Reith, the Director General of the British Broadcasting Corporation. He told Emily and Maisie that all credit was due to them.

Gerard and Emily had a light-hearted, often witty companionship, but she now realised that, even though he would occasionally make love to her, it was only at moments when for an instant he was able to see her as somebody other than herself.

She had been in love with him ever since he had first entered her family's life when she was a little girl of eleven. Not even her beloved Giles had carried quite the same glamorous aura that Gerard had always had for her. She had watched him fall head over heels in love with Alice, and her sister returning his passion, and had accepted then that he would never see her as anything more than a little sister. When Alice died, she realised now that she had been hoping for the impossible, that a fantasy could become a reality. She knew now that this was never going to happen.

She recognised properly for the first time that the love she had shared with Giles had gone far deeper and been more serious than her one-sided romance with Gerard. She would always remain Alice's little sister in Gerard's mind, and he would have felt he was betraying his first love to allow himself to enjoy a true married life with Emily. Her main importance to him now was as a guardian for his daughter, Maisie.

She couldn't blame Gerard, and when he told her that he had decided to rent a small flat in the centre of Liverpool to avoid disturbing her when he was working late, Emily had smiled and said that that was probably a good idea.

15

The Shakespeareans

Manchester – May 1933

Sam Logan and his friend, Bill Hartlepool, were in Sam's room reading *The Merchant of Venice* out loud to each other. They had each been instilled with a passion for Shakespeare by their English master at Manchester High. When they were sixteen, Sir Donald Woolfitt's touring company had come to the Palace Theatre and Sam and Bill had both been to see a production of *The Merchant* and then gone back-stage to meet the great man. Sir Donald had taken enough interest in the two eager young men to listen to them for several minutes while they told him what they thought about the play, and about their own hopes and dreams of becoming actors. They wondered how he thought they should begin....

Then Sir Donald had smiled at them both kindly for a moment, touched by their enthusiasm, before shaking his head gloomily, saying: 'The life of an actor is very, very tough – a constant struggle. Are you prepared to persevere for years and years of poverty and disappointment? Otherwise it should not be attempted.'

Now, in the spring of 1933, Sam and Bill were training to be chartered accountants. Their enthusiasm for Shakespeare had continued since they left school, however, and that summer they were busy preparing their own two-handed version of *The Merchant of Venice* for the Manchester Gala in July. Bill called round at Sam's house in Manchester Road early most mornings so that they could rehearse before they set off to catch their tram for work.

Bill read his Shylock with full-blooded Semitic relish.

'How like a fawning publican he looks!

I hate him for he is a Christian ...'

It was better than trying to do *Hamlet*, where most people knew all the famous speeches by heart and you had half the front row joining in and putting you off. The problem with the *Merchant* was there was really only one decent part, unless you counted Portia, and neither of them liked playing a woman, even one dressed as a man. In the end it was settled that Bill would play Shylock to Sam's Antonio, and then Sam could be Shylock to Bill's Portia. Sam was tall and bony, with dark brown eyes and a large nose, whereas Bill was shorter and red-haired with a smooth round face, and made a better-looking female.

There were always several regulars waiting for the same tram. One was a man with a thin face who would lean his ear against the pole which supported the overhead wires.

'Aye reet, `ere she cooms!' he would say, long before there was any sign of the 82X in the road. He could feel the vibration from the wires as the tram began to climb up from the valley, and minutes after his announcement the 'city-bound ' inward car would soon grind up to the point opposite the stop. As the two young men were walking down the road they could see him in the distance, just turning back to speak to the early morning queue. The two boys started to run, but they were too late. More people were already queuing up for the next tram by the time they arrived.

They waited, Bill muttering under his breath,

> '... *You call me misbeliever, cut-throat dog,*
> *And spit upon my Jewish gaberdine,*
> *And all for use of that which is mine own.*
> *Well, then, it now appears you need my help ...* '

Sam shouted, 'Hang on, here she comes.'

At last they were able to haul themselves up with the rest of the queue in a slow orderly manner into the tramcar, which had a stern sign on the side: *'Intending passengers must form a queue and board cars in that order'*, with the added warning: *'Persons not complying may be prosecuted'.*

The two young men in their dark business suits began to make their way towards the back of the tram, and as they passed the line of seated passengers, Bill greeted a pretty, curly-haired girl wearing school uniform.

''Mornin', Helen. How are we?'

'Hallo, Bill. We don't usually see you on this tram!' She had a deep dimple when she smiled.

'No – we missed ours. Sam, do you know Miss Helen Thorpe? Helen – my pal, Sam Logan.'

'How do you do?' They bowed slightly to each other, and Sam nearly lost his balance as the tram jolted off. Apart from his cousin Maisie, he didn't know any girls near to his own age, and was instantly attracted by the warmth in Helen's bright blue eyes. The girl next to Helen glanced up for one second and caught his eye, then continued to scrawl in her book of homework.

Bill was saying, 'Sam and I are doing Shakespeare at the Town Hall for the Gala, Helen. Will you be there to see us?'

'A two-handed version of *The Merchant of Venice,'* Sam added seriously.

Helen nudged the girl sitting next to her. 'Oh we'll certainly come, won't we, Hazel?'

Her friend looked up at them to reveal slightly prominent front teeth in a grin that lit up a rather solemn face with a small, turned-up nose. She had large, heavy lidded hazel eyes and said, in what Sam thought of as a 'posh' voice, '*The Merchant of Venice* two-handed? However can you do that? Will you have to keep running on and off the stage in different wigs?'

They all laughed and she blushed and returned to her homework.

'Hazel does *elocution*,' said Helen, looking proudly at her friend who shook her head, frowning. 'She does recitations on the stage at our school at the end of term. Bill, you must call round and tell Mother about the Gala. She'll want to know there's a famous actor living next door!'

'Ha! Well, we'd better be moving along.'

More passengers were crowding on and Sam and Bill were pushed on down the tram.

'Who is the girl with Helen?' Sam whispered to Bill when they were far enough away.

'Hazel Lancashire,' Bill whispered back. 'You know – the Lancashires? – the jewellers? They are all a cut above the likes of us. But she and Helen are great pals.'

'Do you know Helen well?'

'Well – you know – we're neighbours. Come on. We're there.'

The boys struggled back down the tram, smiling at the girls as they passed them. Helen gave them a little wave.

A week later the two young men once again travelled into the city centre on the same tram as the girls. Hazel was reading a book, but she looked up again with her shy grin as the boys came up and said 'Hallo'.

Sam smiled back.

'How long until your holidays begin?' Bill asked Helen.

'Just another week. Hurray! And then, of course, it will be time for your Gala! We are both coming to watch you aren't we, Hazel?'

'It will be the highlight of our holidays,' Hazel said solemnly.

'Don't frighten us more than we already are!'

'If you are frightened by a couple of schoolgirls in the audience, I don't think your acting careers are going to last very long.'

As the two young men were walking down past the girls to get off the tram, Sam dropped a note into Hazel's satchel that was on the floor at her feet:

Dear Miss Lancashire,

Would you come to the pictures with me next Saturday? I'll wait for you outside the Savoy Heaton Moor at six o'clock. Sam.

PS I hope you like Laurel and Hardy

Hazel stared after him; then she showed the note to Helen.

'You must have clicked!' Helen said laughing. 'Will you go?'

'No! I hardly know him! You wouldn't, would you?'

'Oh yes I would. Sam seems very nice. And he is sure to be nice if he's a pal of Bill Hartlepool.'

'But *Laurel and Hardy!* I ask you!' They both started to giggle. 'I wonder why he's asked me. You're the one he kept looking at.'

'Don't be soft. You've clicked! Do go, Hazel. It would be such a thing.'

On the following Saturday, Hazel woke up with hay fever and was sneezing and coughing all morning. In the afternoon she summoned her younger brother, Alan, and told him to cycle down to the cinema in Heaton Moor with a note she had written for a gentleman who he would find standing outside waiting for her. Cycling over to the cinema Alan saw a tall, thin, dark-haired man with a big nose standing outside on the pavement looking anxiously up and down. He peddled over to him and coming to a halt, balancing on tip toe to keep his bike upright, he said brightly, 'Hallo?'

Sam glanced at him, but didn't answer. Alan stared at him uncertainly for a few seconds, then asked, 'Are you waiting for my sister Hazel?'

Sam realised the strange boy was talking to him. He said eagerly,

'Oh, yes. Yes, I am. Is she coming?'

Alan silently handed Sam Hazel's note.

Dear Sam,

I am very sorry but I have a very bad hay fever and can't come out with you this evening. Perhaps you would call here for tea on Saturday week when I'm better, and then we might go to the cinema another time.

Yours sincerely,

Hazel Lancashire.

PS Could it not be Laurel and Hardy?

Alan was already peddling energetically away up the road, bottom in the air when Sam looked up to thank him. Sam walked slowly and sadly into the cinema alone with his two tickets, but was soon chuckling admiringly at the ingenious antics of his two heroes.

*

Hazel Lancashire's family lived in a large stone farmhouse on top of a high hill. Sam left Manchester by tram, and at Whaley Bridge got off and walked for a mile beside the Leeds and Liverpool Canal. He hesitated for a moment at the bottom of a winding road that seemed to be the main way up to Hazel's house, before deciding to take a well-worn track that led directly up the hill across a field of sheep. As he climbed cautiously over the style in his best clothes, the quietly grazing sheep looked up in simultaneous alarm, then scattered bleating to a far corner of the field, where they turned as one and stared at him.

Arriving slightly breathless at the top of the field he climbed over the gate and made his way round a row of small farm cottages into a muddy farmyard with a big new square brick building to the left that he decided would be the working farmer's house. Hazel's family home was of stone, the same age as the cottages, and stood a little apart from the rest, overlooking the great valley. He inspected his shoes and tried to wipe some of the mud off on the grass verge outside the gate.

There appeared to be only one accessible door, and as soon as he knocked it was opened by the same boy who had brought him the note. The door opened directly into a large, family kitchen. Over Alan's head Sam could see other members of the family sitting round a big pine wood table. There was no sign of Hazel, but Sam was greeted kindly by her mother, Muriel, who had been standing at the range watching a large pot of water coming to the boil.

'The watched pot never boils!' she said laughing, turning round and shaking Sam warmly by the hand.

'How do you do, Mrs Lancashire.'

'Welcome, Sam. Hazel has told us all about you. I gather you and young Alan have already met. But I don't think you know my younger daughter, Jenny?'

Sam bowed to Jenny, who looked very like Hazel, but was perhaps a year or two younger. She was peeling potatoes into a bowl at the table. She had a beautiful smile, which she bestowed serenely on him before returning to her chore. Jenny had more delicate features than her sister but, Sam thought, her face seemed to lack some of Hazel's humour and animation.

'And this is Jimmy, our youngest.'

'Very pleased to meet you, Master James,' Sam said formally, shaking Jimmy's hand. Mrs Lancashire laughed and Jimmy and Alan both giggled.

'My elder sons are washing and changing because they'll be off to the cinema after tea. Hazel must be about somewhere. Go and see if she's out in the garden, Sam. She'll be hiding away somewhere reading her novel, if I know my daughter.'

'I'll show you,' said Alan jumping down from the table.

Alan led Sam out of the back door and down a path round the house leading into a big garden, with an apple orchard surrounded by walls and hedges. He found Hazel perched in a hole in the hedge, deeply engrossed in a book.

'Hallo, Hazel, is your cold better?'

Hazel quickly put the book under her bottom when she saw Sam approaching, and climbed out to greet him. When she stood up she was much taller than he had realised from seeing her sitting on the tram – barely two inches shorter than he was.

'Yes thank you. Much better. It was only hay fever.'

Sam bent down to pick up her book and quickly looked at the title. He grinned at her.

'Aha. A saucy novel!'

She frowned. 'A *romantic* novel,' she corrected him firmly. 'Helen lent it to me because I was under par. I don't usually read things like this, but it is rather amusing.'

They walked back to the kitchen together, where her two elder brothers, Tom and Frank had now joined the family group. Sam said, 'I found your daughter hiding in the hedge, just as you said, Mrs Lancashire .... And furthermore, reading a saucy novel by Eleanor Glyn.'

'Oh! You fibber! I was reading a *romantic* novel, by Ethel M. Drew.'

Sam shook his head gravely.

Muriel Lancashire and the two older boys laughed. She wagged her finger at Hazel. 'What will Sam think of us, Hazel? Sam, dear, I want you to meet Tom and Frank.'

As he shook hands with Hazel's elder brothers, Sam noticed that all the members of her family had the same Manchester accent as his own family, and only Hazel spoke with what he thought of as 'grand' vowel sounds. It would be up to him to impress Hazel if he ever wanted to ... He thought Hazel's voice was beautiful, her eyes were beautiful, her tall, skinny body was beautiful and she was beautiful. 'That's the girl I'm going to marry,' he promised himself as he went back home after tea.

*

Hazel was a popular young lady and already had several admirers. One of them, David Barrett, returned home from Leeds where he was a medical student on the day of the Manchester Gala, and he and his brother joined Hazel and her best friend, Helen, who were also with a group of their friends from school. Leo, too, had come to watch Sam perform and brought his fiancé, Martha, while Freddy, Clifford and Philip were sitting together in another part of the hall with some of their own friends.

Just before the interval, Sam and Bill performed their two-handed *Merchant of Venice* to great acclaim and only forgot their lines twice, when they had to do a quick scene change and character switch. Everyone laughed at Bill's portrayal of Portia, and both their Shylocks were greeted with cheers and loud applause. During the interval people came over to shake their hands and congratulate them with big grins. Sam's brothers came up beaming and shook his hands. 'You've done us proud, our Sam!'

When Sam and Bill joined their friends in the tea bar at the back of the theatre, a talking contest began. The two young actors both wanted to re-live their experience by telling everyone all the terrors and triumphs that they had endured on stage. David of course only wanted to talk to Hazel, whom he hadn't seen for some weeks; he and Sam both directed their conversation towards her, competing for her attention.

'I think I had better cut along home now,' David said to Hazel after a while. 'I must go and see my mother, if you'll all excuse us. I haven't even had a chance to say "hallo" yet, because I came straight here. I'll come round to your house tomorrow and we can make some proper plans.'

Hazel smiled her toothy grin, and she and Helen exchanged a private glance as David and his brother stood up and shook hands with Sam and Bill and congratulated them again, before going out into the sunny street. Sam turned to Hazel. 'May I escort you home, Hazel?'

'Oh thank you, kind sir!'

As she stood up to leave with him she threw a Helen a private look. They walked towards the bus stop. After a slight pause she said, 'So when are you going to become a famous actor, Sam?'

'That was only a dream. I really wanted to study law....'

'More than becoming a famous actor?'

He laughed. 'Well, it would be work for "a man of ambition". But I think I'm probably more suited to accountancy.'

'It sounds so awfully dull.'

'It isn't a bit dull! It's far too difficult! It's like having to solve a series of very difficult puzzles. Just when you think you've answered one question, you find a whole lot of other things now come out wrong, so you have to start all over again.'

Hazel yawned, and smiled at him. 'Mmm.'

'Oh well. How can you expect a girl who hides in the hedge reading Eleanor Glyn novels to understand?'

'Oh! You liar! I have never ever read her silly books.'

Sam looked up at the sky and whistled cheerfully. Hazel thumped him.

16

Sam and Hazel

Manchester – August 1936

For the past six months Sam had been working down in Wolverhampton for a firm of accountants for the final year of his training. It was too far to come home every weekend so he was living in digs, only managing to travel back north once a month. He and Hazel had exchanged letters while he was away, but he had only seen her twice.

Hazel belonged to a hiking club which included her two elder brothers and their girlfriends, as well as Hazel's best friend, Helen and their friends, David and Robert Barrett. They were planning a long hike to the Lake District over the August Bank Holiday weekend, staying in a YMCA on Saturday night. Hazel had written to tell Sam about it, but although Sam was due home that weekend, he always had a Saturday morning job for Gerard Belringer in Manchester whenever he was home, so he said that he wouldn't be able to join them.

Late that Saturday afternoon, when Hazel and the hiking club were all resting on a grassy hillside beside the road, Sam suddenly appeared puffing up the hill towards them on his bike.

After giving a loud shout of triumph when he realised he'd caught up with them, he collapsed on the grass in an exhausted heap.

Everyone laughed and congratulated him; then Hazel said rather crossly that he couldn't come along with them any further as he had a bike so he'd had a pointless journey.

She only told him much later that it was at that moment she had decided she would marry him.

Wolverhampton – April 1937

Six months later, Sam passed his final accountancy exams and received the results while he was still living in Wolverhampton. He didn't smoke or drink, and felt at a loss as to how to celebrate his great achievement. He went downstairs to show his landlady his letter, and she patted him on the back and gave him a glass of homemade lemonade. In desperation, he went out and bought himself a packet of cigarettes. His first experimental puff, as he sat on a bench outside the tobacconists, made him choke, but he understood in that instant that smoking was going to be for him.

Manchester – May 1937

When Sam got home, he invited Hazel to meet his parents for the first time. He met her off the tram, and they walked together along Manchester Road, entering through a gate in a tall hedgerow that led to a brick path up to Sam's house, with rows of vegetables planted in raised beds all along one side.

'What are those things for?' Hazel asked, pointing. Sam didn't reply.

'Look. There. What are those upside-down flower pots on poles for?'

'I *am* looking – I'm thinking ... I don't know ... to trap snails?'

Hazel frowned doubtfully. 'They wouldn't make a very good trap. Wouldn't all the snails turn round and slide out again?'

'We'll ask my father. He's the gardener.'

As Sam opened the back door, they could hear the faint sound of a piano coming from a distant room, and someone singing a popular song in a pleasant bass baritone.

Sam led Hazel into the kitchen where Leah was standing at a large wooden table pounding dough with some force. She was talking to someone who Hazel couldn't see at first, until she realised that in the corner of the room there was a man sitting by the range trying to read his newspaper. A big brown dog came over and began sniffing Hazel's coat suspiciously.

'You should have done it years ago, Will – we all begged you. Now what will happen? I don't think I could ...' Leah broke off when she became aware of Sam and Hazel standing in the kitchen doorway, and she turned to greet them with a polite, welcoming smile.

'Ah, so our Sam has finally brought his mystery young lady home to meet us! Why ever did you not bring Miss Lancashire to the front door, Sam?' Hazel was appraised by a pair of shrewd grey eyes, and then she found herself being pulled round, her hands seized in a warm grasp by Sam's father, who had risen swiftly from his seat by the fire.

'Welcome, welcome, my dear!' he said with a wide smile, gazing at her with a pair of twinkling brown eyes before kissing her on both cheeks.

'This is Miss Lancashire, Mother. Hazel, please meet my mother and father. Get down, Juno.' Sam pushed away the dog still sniffing at the hem of Hazel's coat.

Hazel, her two hands clasped by Sam's father, smiled from one to the other.

'I've been so looking forward to meeting you. My mother asks to be remembered to you, Mrs Logan. She tells me she met you at a concert party a little while ago, where she had so much enjoyed your singing.'

'Now that is so kind of her, isn't it? Sam, you take your Miss Lancashire upstairs until your father and I are ready in the parlour to welcome her properly. And on your way up, please tell Clifford I need him down here *now* please.'

Sam and Hazel trooped out through a dark passageway and up the front staircase.

'I fear that "welcoming you properly" means giving you an enormous tea,' Sam whispered. Hazel grinned. On the first floor Sam knocked on a door that immediately flew open to reveal a bedroom with three beds in it. Standing in the doorway there was a young man with his head down, holding a camera to his chest. Clicking it, he took a picture of their startled faces. When he raised his head, Hazel found herself being assessed by a pair of amused grey eyes. She thought there was something calculating in his expression that Sam's innocent face never had.

'Mother wants to see you downstairs at once, Clifford,' Sam said, and immediately began to walk on.

'Aren't you going to introduce me to your young lady, Sam?'

'This is my brother, Clifford. Clifford, this is Miss Hazel Lancashire. Mother is waiting.'

Clifford made an exaggerated bow to Hazel, and Sam led her on up another, darker flight of stairs and then another, even narrower flight, into a big attic room. There were piles of books all over the floor, and old school exercise books strewn across various tables. Around the room were boxes of coins and old keys, fishing rods, a tent, a kite, an old crystal radio set, and a newer radio cabinet with a large horn, beside a large box of gramophone records. Someone had made a child's wooden car out of a dismantled book case. There was an easel and round the walls were displays of photographs and watercolours, all clearly the work of the room's usual occupants. Hazel went first to the window to admire the view of the garden far down below, before walking slowly round the room peering curiously at everything. She glanced at Sam, lounging on a low chair, his long legs stretched out in front of him, watching her as she made her inspection.

'I like your father, Sam.'

'Everyone loves my father. He is a dear man.'

'Your mother seems a bit … daunting?'

'Oh, Mother is wonderful, but she is very protective of her family, and she is deeply suspicious of any young ladies we bring home. Unlike my father, who welcomes them a bit too much sometimes!' Hazel smiled, and he looked back at her seriously.

'How many brothers did you say you have?'

'Six. Our only sister, Molly, died in the war of diphtheria when she was a baby. So – now there are just seven of us, Albert and Edgar, the two eldest – who are both married – then there's Leo, who you've met and is engaged to Martha, then Philip, Clifford, *me,* and Freddy, the youngest. Freddy is the one we heard singing when we came in. He is very serious about his music and has got by far the best voice of all of us. I entered a national singing competition myself once. But I found nobody had told me what to do with my hands! Wherever I put them they seemed to be in the way.'

He demonstrated – pulling a funny face and rapidly moving is hands first behind his back, then crossed together in front, then on his hips and, finally, down to attention. Hazel laughed, 'I hope you won after all that!'

'No. But they gave me a certificate for fifth place. I gave up after that. Now – have you noticed the watercolours? Leo has done most of them. But Albert is pretty good at drawing too – he's more of a photographer though.'

'Leo is …?'

'Third eldest. He works as a draftsman for the Council. Look at this beautiful tree he's painted – it's of the one just outside our front door. I never realised how many colours there are in the trunk of a tree. I would probably just have used shades of brown and perhaps green and black – but look at Leo's, he hasn't used any brown at all, there's white and yellow and green and gold and red and purple and black – and yet it still looks like a brown tree trunk. Leo may call in later. He usually does.'

'So you're the second youngest ... and Clifford – is he the one just above you?'

Sam looked suddenly serious. 'Yes. But I'm afraid Clifford is rather a rascal. You need to watch out for him.'

'Goodness! How exciting! Is that why you've never introduced me to your family before? Dark secrets?'

'No. But – well – I didn't want to barge in where I wasn't wanted ... you have at least one other admirer, do you not? One of many, I suspect.'

Hazel blushed and said hurriedly, 'Oh David Barrett isn't really an admirer. Well, perhaps a little. But only ...' She broke off, not sure what she wanted to say about David. She had definitely decided that she preferred Sam, mainly because he could make her laugh, and he didn't make her feel inferior as David sometimes did, just by being so *good.* And David was away for such a long time studying. *And* he was a vegetarian. She sighed, feeling dissatisfied with herself.

Sam had been watching her closely, and now he laughed. 'Your face is a picture! Now, to finish the guided tour of my family tree – all my brothers are charming, even our Clifford, although Albert, the eldest, is the *most* charming, except he always seems to be doing something daft. He's a very good amateur photographer, and only the other day he saw a rare bird out of this window, so he ran downstairs to find his camera, then came running back up here and stuck his head straight through the glass ... He nearly knocked himself out, but he just kept saying, "That window was open a second ago!"

They both laughed, and Sam went on, 'Edgar is the clever business man of the family. He's got his own motor-car repair business now. Philip used to work for him, but he's branched out into motor bikes and motor cycles. The three eldest are all married and have young families. You aren't supposed to have a favourite, and Albert and Edgar and Philip are all very nice, but Leo is the one I admire the most. He's very sensitive and artistic. And Freddy is ... well, we are great pals. We are all quite close. My father was ... ill ... and had to be away for a long time during the war, so my eldest brothers had to leave school early to help feed the family. My sister and Freddy and Clifford and I were all still too young to be of much use.'

'*My* father got TB during the war. He actually died of it later – just two years ago, actually.'

'Yes, I know. I'm sorry.'

'For years he had to spend six months every winter in Switzerland, so I hardly knew him, but it was very hard on my mother. She had to supervise the shops as well as look after us children. But even when Daddy came home, I didn't like it, because he would take up all her time and attention. I went with her in a taxi to meet him at the station once. As soon as he got in he began hugging and kissing my mother and I heard him say, "Why did you have to bring the brat along?" ... I am afraid ... I was ... glad when he died.'

She waited, expecting him to say something, but he just looked at her seriously and remained silent. She went on. 'My two elder brothers are a bit resentful, because, like your family, they had to leave school early to work in the shops with Daddy away so much of the time. Tom wanted to be a lawyer – like you did – but now he runs one of the shops and Frank runs the other one. Alan and Jimmy are both learning to be farmers, and, as you know, Jenny and I have got the little baby clothes shop in Cheadle. So that's my family story.'

After a pause Sam said, 'Please tell me something about your Jenny. Is there something the matter with her?'

Hazel sighed. 'Yes. Jenny has epilepsy. She was all right when she was younger, but as she's grown older – since she was a teenager, she's started having these fits. Some days she's still fine and Mother hopes she'll grow out of it but I ... well I don't know.'

'I am sorry. She is always so gentle and sweet.' Sam looked at his watch. 'Well. Let's go down. I expect Mother will be ready to "receive you properly" by now.'

Hazel followed him back down the three flights of stairs to the ground floor. William was just coming out of the dining room into the front hall, but stopped and turned back when he saw them, saying, 'Ah there you both are, my dears. Come in, come in. I was just coming up to find you.'

The dining room was dark even on a summer's day – a long narrow room lit only by the north-facing window onto the garden at the far end. An enormously long oak table nearly filled the room, with big carved chairs down either side. The table had been laid with a white cloth weighed down with plates of fruit cake, bread and butter and a big bowl of tomatoes.

Clifford came in bearing an enormous tea-pot, followed by his mother carrying a tray of sandwiches and another with more bread and butter. Another young man followed them, pushing a trolley on which there were six plates of salmon and boiled potatoes.

'Thank you, Frederick. Miss Lancashire, please would you sit down at the end there, next to Samuel's father.'

Hazel squeezed herself behind the row of chairs to sit next to Mr Logan who was already seated at the head of the table, his back to the window. Clifford made as though to sit next to her, but his mother checked him and Samuel moved quickly down the row, giving his brother a cold stare.

'Have you met our youngest son, Frederick, Miss Lancashire?'

'Please call me Hazel, Mrs Logan. No, I don't think so – but I heard you singing very beautifully just now. It was lovely.'

Freddy blushed and said, 'I saw you at the Gala.' He smiled, and gave her a little bow.

After they had eaten all the bread and butter, the plates of hot salmon and potato were passed down the table. This was followed by slices of fruit cake, and then Leah and Frederick went out and returned with a bowl of custard and an enormous apple pie decorated with pastry flowers. Hazel looked at these new arrivals on the table with an expression of such fear that both Sam and his father, who had been watching to see her reaction, laughed at her discomfort.

'We enjoy our tea in this family, my dear,' William said, patting her hand. 'But don't you worry. We will only be having another three courses! Now what will you have?'

'I'm so sorry, Mrs Logan, but I fear I couldn't manage another morsel.'

'Well I know plenty here who will,' said Leah comfortably from the other end of the table. At that moment two more faces, older versions of Samuel's, appeared at the door.

'Why are you all in the dining room?' said one of them. 'Have we got a visitor?'

'Albert! Eddie! Come and meet Samuel's Miss Lancashire. Miss Lancashire, these are our two eldest sons, Albert and Edgar,' said Mrs Logan with pride, and then hurried out to return with two more plates of hot salmon and potato. The two men sat down and smiled at Hazel.

'Ah, it's the famous Miss Lancashire! At long last, after hearing so much about you! No wonder we are dining in style tonight.'

Hazel smiled at them. While William explained the purpose of upside-down flower pots and other garden lore to Hazel and Sam, Sam's elder brothers began talking in quiet urgent voices to their mother at the other end of the table. Hazel heard Edgar saying, 'He has to do it, Mother ...' but then he lowered his voice and she couldn't hear the rest of the sentence. Then she heard Albert, the other brother, say, 'Yes, but we can't count on Belringer being able to help us this time,' and Mrs Logan said, 'Oh, I'm sure it won't come to that.'

William saw that Hazel's attention was being distracted from his explanation of the intricacies of creating a perfect lawn and said, 'I'm afraid I'm boring you, Miss Lancashire.'

'Oh! No! No, not at all. It was just I ...'

'I know. We all want to know what they were talking about so earnestly down there.' He looked along at his wife and sons, and raised his voice, 'You are making Miss Lancashire and me curious, with all your wise heads muttering together down there.'

Edgar said to Hazel, 'Do your brothers think there is going to be another war, Miss Lancashire?'

'Oh no,' said Hazel. 'I mean, I expect *they* do. They are always talking about all the awful rumours in the papers – but *I'm* quite sure there can't be. Not again.'

'My sentiments exactly,' said William. 'We must believe and trust that goodness and common sense will prevail in the end. But my family are worried, Miss Lancashire, because I, as young Sam here will no doubt have told you, happen to have been born in Hamburg and so, although I have lived here all my life, my beloved mother and father were German and I, too, am German.'

Hazel stared at him. 'But you don't sound ...'

'No. I can sing in German but the funny thing is, I can't speak it – or not very well. My sons want me to adopt British nationality so that I won't be regarded as an enemy in your beautiful country. And believe me, my dear, I do quite understand how you might feel – your own father was a hero of the last war, Sam tells me, and I know of so many other heroic young men who lost their lives. Even now the streets of Manchester are crowded with too many brave young men who were wounded and are now unable to find work. But believe me, my family suffered too. They nearly starved, Miss Lancashire, with their only bread-winner a prisoner on the Isle of Man. My little daughter died. Your young man, Sam here, very nearly died too.'

Hazel appeared to have been shocked speechless. 'I hadn't told Miss Lancashire any of this, Father,' said Sam.

'Sam has only told me you were from Liverpool, Mr Logan.'

'Liverpool is where my parents came to live, where I grew up, and where I met my beautiful Leah.'

He smiled at his wife at the far end of the table, who shook her head grimly. 'I was a babe in arms when we came to live here. My dear father always said I was to think of myself as "a citizen of the world." That was his great idea – that we should all be citizens of the world, and not make a fuss about belonging to one nation or another.'

'Yes, well, but it isn't just *you* we have to worry about, is it, Father?' Clifford said suddenly. 'If there is to be another war with Germany, we might all be rounded up as enemy aliens this time.'

William looked sadly round at his family and everyone started to make protesting remarks at once.

'Don't be foolish, Clifford,' Edgar said sharply. 'Of course it won't come to that. But I do wish you would think seriously about becoming naturalised, Father – if only for Mother's sake.'

William shook his head sadly. 'It is a little late for that now.'

'I am so sorry if you think I was rude, Mr Logan,' Hazel said. 'But I never – I mean, I always thought Germans … I mean my father wasn't really a hero or anything. He did get tuberculosis because of the war, but I don't think he got any nearer to France than Caterham. I don't think I've ever met a real German before, and I don't know anything about … your country.'

'Germany is very beautiful – but it isn't mine. I have only visited it only once in my life, two or three years ago, when I travelled to Leipzig on business and I went to Dresden because I had heard it so much about its beauty.'

'Is it as beautiful as people say?'

'Yes. Exceptionally beautiful. I only wish Leo could have been with me to draw it. It is like two cities rolled into one – old, romantic, medieval, Dresden with some wonderful baroque churches, as well as a very attractive modern city. Let us just hope that you and I are both right, Miss Lancashire, and there will be no such madness as another war.'

17

'Peace in Our Time'

Manchester – July 1937

William was a prolific letter writer. He wrote regularly to young authors to encourage them, and weekly letters to his sons whenever they were away from home. The one person he had not been able to keep in touch with, because none of them had an address for him, was his younger brother, Freddie. Then in July 1937, he received the first news they had had from Freddie since he had disappeared from view shortly after Otto's death:

98 London Road, Sevenoaks, Kent,

Tubs Hill Pharmacy Freddie Logan MPS.

Phone 1099

Dear William,

You will no doubt be surprised to hear from me after so long. I write to tell you my news. After many years of working hard, I have now, through careful containment of my resources, been able to purchase my own business, a chemist shop, Tubbs Hill

Pharmacy, and I have been elected a Member of the Pharmaceutical Society.

Even happier news is that I have met and married a charming lady called Edith, and we have a delightful 9-year old daughter, both of whom I hope to introduce to the family before long. Mary-Ann is much younger than any of her cousins, but she is very like young Maisie, who I remember so well as a lively five-year old.

It is Sunday morning & I have just come back from a four-mile walk through the woods of the Knole estate close by. In the centre of this wood is a tree on which many years ago someone carved these words – 'Alice, Forget-me-not.'

But then, how could one? Certainly not I.

Freddie

William silently passed the letter over to Leah, who read it frowning, then looked up at William. 'Well I never! He always was such a curious young man.'

'Yes – what a funny chap Freddie is! He was always rather secretive so I never really know what is going on in his head. At least he seems to have found some happiness. I'm glad. I must show this to Emily. She'll want to write to him.'

Liverpool – October 1937

Gerard Belringer had taken a great interest in Sam's career ever since he started his accountancy training, and recently had begun introducing him to some of his business acquaintances. Sam's first job before he had qualified was working as a clerk on Saturday mornings for Gerard's new Belringer radio company. Now he was qualified, his first professional audit was also being done for Gerard.

'I've been rather reluctant to look too closely myself at where I stand these days, Sam,' Gerard said apologetically. 'You'll probably find things a bit confusing.'

Gerard had invested his money in a wide variety of enterprises as well as in his own radio marketing company. There had been a big economic boom after the war ended, but that had been followed by a crash and a long depression. Gerard himself hadn't done too badly. His investments were nearly all in small enterprises that, despite of the downturn, were still slowly growing, as in the case of Albert and Edgar's motor-car servicing business and his own radio company. Gerard also received income as a journalist as well as an adviser to several international corporations, including Marconi. His contacts in America and with the BBC gave him access to several important people who in turn gave him a great deal of useful information that he could pass on to his clients. In spite of this, as

Sam quickly realised, Gerard was still living on credit most of the time.

'I know what you are going to say, Sam. You are going to tell me what my wife is always saying – that I must cut back on my expenses.'

'No, Gerard, I'm not going to say that. I think your impressive life-style is part of your modus operandi. I've seen it's how you get your uncanny feel for the zeitgeist and I don't believe you would be nearly so effective without it. I am no gambler myself, but I agree with your somewhat Keynesian approach to your own affairs. Your real problem is that everyone you do business with is profiting from your unique advisory skills – except you! I am quite serious, Gerard. You are simply not charging enough! I notice, for example, that you have never received anything at all from the Liberal party.'

Gerard laughed delightedly. Then he became serious again. 'Well, no, I don't charge the Liberals. I never have. But as for everything else – well that's the part I hate, Sam – talking about money. I keep putting it off and then when I have to do it I always think it sounds far too much.'

Sam said earnestly, 'From now on you must assess how much work you are likely to be asked to do for each client, how much time it will take, how many meetings they'll want you attend, how many visits to London or America – these are all real costs to you, not only all your entertainment expenses. Add that all up, add ten percent, and then double it. It should come to at least four times what you are garnering at the moment. These people you are advising do know your value – they won't stop coming to you just because you charge proper rates for your unique, highly specialised and professional advice. I don't believe they will even blink.'

'My God, Sam! Are you sure?'

'Of course I'm sure. Look – I've made a chart of all the charges made by other professions – lawyers, accountants, doctors, tax advisers and so forth. Your fees don't come anywhere near any of them. '

'I see! Golly! But I still think I am going to have to spend a long time standing in front of a mirror practising saying to Lord Greenaway, "My charge will be *fifty pounds!*" I won't be able to keep a straight face! But thank you, Sam! I knew you were the man for me!'

'The only other small query I have, Gerard, is about you paying for the upkeep of this other Liverpool residence. You seem to be paying rather a lot for a flat but receiving no income from it. Is that …?

'Absolutely necessary, Sam. I have a sick relative living there who I am supporting.'

'Oh I'm sorry. Yes of course.'

In 1935 Tommy Rea had retired from managing his Manchester bookshop, and proposed that William should take over.
William, ever since his return from Leipzig, had already decided he was ready to leave Chapman and Hall after nearly twenty
years, and had accepted with alacrity. He said to Leah, 'The
part of my job I enjoy most these days is encouraging young
writers. I can do that just as well from the bookshop, and I'll
have more time to think.'

'I think it is because you'll have more time to enjoy writing
your long fatherly letters to young women, Wills!'

He smiled. 'But, Leah, they are the ones who are writing all
the interesting books these days. They want to write about the
world about them, the things they know about, without trying
to come up with all sorts of fancy clever-clever notions.'

'Just so long as you aren't giving them false hopes, Will.'

One of the young would-be authors he had been writing to
every week for several years was his sister's daughter, Maisie,
who was dreaming of becoming a writer, and sometimes sent
him little poems she had written, but wasn't sure how to begin
writing a book. Now he suggested that she should come and
work for him in the bookshop so they could put their heads

together to discuss ideas. Almost as soon as Maisie arrived in Manchester, they had come up with what they both thought would be the perfect project for her start on.

'Write about what you know,' William was always saying to her, 'that was why the original publishing company I worked for was so successful. It was all done by local authors writing about the local scene.' She was looking at him one day as he said this yet again, and then they both said simultaneously 'Our family!'

Manchester – January 1938

With William's encouragement, Maisie, now aged twenty-three, was researching Otto and Anna's early life, getting her father and Emily as well as William and Leah to tell her all they could remember. Gerard told her several stories that made Maisie laugh, especially ones about Anna's loud exclamations at the peculiarities of the English. William introduced her to Tommy Rea, who took her to see his now elderly father, Harry, who had been Otto's best friend for so many years. Harry spoke to Maisie about her grandfather with so much love and admiration that she was more enthusiastic than ever about writing their story.

She had learned German at school, but now she decided that she wanted to learn more about the language and the culture.

She had been particularly excited to discover that Otto's mother's maiden name was Mendelssohn. 'It would certainly be a good connection to have when it comes to finding a publisher!' William told her. 'You could call it: *I was Mendelssohn's Cousin!*'

In her great-aunt Clara's friendship book that Emily had kept, Maisie found the addresses of two Mendelssohn families living in Hamburg. In May she wrote to them both in her careful school-girl German, telling them about her grandfather's side of her family in England, and asking if she could meet them. One of them replied immediately to say that they must be cousins, and that she would be very welcome to visit them. Maisie decided she must go to Germany as soon as possible to meet them. She also had Hans and Shirley's new address since they had moved to Berlin, and she planned to visit them and meet all the remaining members of Anna's family while she was over there, before returning home in October.

Gerard tried hard to discourage her. 'My darling, darling Maisie, please don't do anything so silly. Germany is no place for foreigners these days. Chancellor Hitler is as insane as the old Kaiser – more insane. He has virtually made himself dictator. They are no longer even part of the League of Nations – if anything happened to you over there, I might not be able to come and rescue you.'

'But we have family over there, Father. I do so want to do this – and if I'm to become a real writer I must be prepared to take some risks. And this will make the story even more exciting.'

'No, Maisie. It's too dangerous. Why not at least start your writing here? I know one very important secret none of the family knows – but I'll only tell you if you promise not to go. Please, my darling, I do know what I'm talking about. Some people are trying to get rid of this mad Chancellor. There's bound to be trouble and I don't want you caught up in it. We'll go over together when things are back to normal and I can show you where to find all the old records. I am a world expert at that!'

Maisie laughed. 'I'd like that too, Father. I'd love us all to go. But I do so want to meet the Mendelssohns now I've made contact with them! Please don't worry about me, Old Thing! I promise you I'll come straight back if there's any sign of trouble…. Now what's this great secret you've been hiding?'

'I won't tell you unless you promise not to go. I'm very angry with your uncle for encouraging this foolish escapade. I suppose I can't stop you if your heart is really set on it, but please keep very alert and please, Maisie, don't get involved with anything political. You must be very, very careful who you talk to over there. I know how you love to take care of beggars and stray cats, but please remember that over there you can't be the one who rescues everybody else. I will be worried sick all the time you are away.'

*

The Old Farm, Whaley Bridge – 24 April 1938
Hazel received a card from Sam on her twenty-second birthday. Inside he had written: *'No sweethearts, I b'lieve?'*

She showed it to her mother, who laughed and said, 'Sam is such a dear, Hazel! What are you going to say back?'

'Only one thing I can say, Mother.... *Barkis is willing!'*

*

Methodist Chapel, Marple – Friday 30 July 1938
Hazel was late. Sam looked anxiously at his watch – it was gone nine – he turned to Muriel Lancashire, who was waiting outside the chapel with him. She smiled and shook her head. 'Hazel will be here, never you fear. You go inside now, Sam.'

Hazel's brothers were sitting stiffly and silently side by side on the front wooden bench on one side of the chapel with Hazel's friend Helen on her own in the row behind; Gerard, Emily and Maisie, William and Leah, with Sam's brothers and their wives and children, filled up some of the pews on the other side of the aisle.

At last a car arrived and Hazel got out. She was wearing a smart two-piece suit with a little hat and holding a spray of flowers. Muriel stepped forward, peering into the car. 'Where's Jenny?' Mother and daughter looked at one another.

'The doctor's with her. He's taking her down to the hospital.' Hazel held up her right hand which was wrapped in a bandage. 'It's only a small bite. The doctor gave me an injection. I'm sorry Jenny will miss my wedding though.'

'Oh dear.'

They went inside together, and the organ began to play. When Hazel reached him, Sam put his arm around her. 'Are you all right? What happened to you? I've been so worried.'

'I'm perfectly all right. It's nothing.' She gave him her funny, toothy grin. 'Sorry to keep you waiting!'

After the ceremony, the two families shared a wedding breakfast at the local hotel, and then Sam and Hazel travelled down to Torquay by train for their honeymoon.

After they had been shown their bedroom with its view of the sea, Sam went down to the bar and ordered two green Chartreuse cocktails, which Gerard had told him would be a suitable drink to offer a young lady in an hotel bar.

'*How* much?'

Sam looked round and could just see Hazel standing outside on the veranda catching the sun, still warm in the early evening. She turned her head a little and he could see she was smiling to herself.

'Well – all right. Would you bring them outside for us, please?'

'Certainly, Sir.' The bar tender spooned crushed ice into two tiny glasses before tipping in a dribble of green, sticky liquid into which he inserted two straws. He placed the glasses on a silver tray and following Sam out onto the veranda put them down in front of them on a glass topped wicker table.

'This is so glamorous, Sam,' Hazel, sitting on a large wicker armchair beside him, stretched out her arms and legs luxuriously.

Sam was looking critically at his glass. 'There doesn't seem to be very much in it,' he said doubtfully.

Hazel picked up her own glass and sipped it.

'Mmm! Delicious.' She sucked up the rest through her straw and handed him her glass imperiously. 'More please!'

Sam tasted his – then handed it to her. 'You have mine. I'll stick to beer.'

Over dinner Sam said, 'Do you think you could teach me to speak like you do? You have such a nice voice and sound like those people on Gerard's radio. I think it would help me in business if I could speak like you.'

Hazel laughed, 'Of course I will, Sam. You've got a good ear so it will be quite easy. It's only a question of the vowel sounds. So – you pronounce this as *booter* and I call it *butter*. Later on, you will be going to have a *bath* but I'll be having a *barth*. I learnt how to do it in my elocution lessons at school: the King's English. I wanted to be an actress when I was young.' She grinned at him. 'Like you! Only – I had stay at home to help Mother with Jenny, and so we ran this little shop together.'

Later that night Sam watched in amazement as Hazel danced round their hotel bedroom, jumping on and off their twin beds, singing, 'I am the dancing nut-cracker – I am the world famous ballerina Hazel Nut!'

*

Hamburg – September 1938

'Am having a splendid time and plenty of practice in the language for we speak German all the time and I seem to be causing a great deal of amusement with my mistakes. I hope you have had a fine weather for your holiday. Tell uncle William – we are all related to the great Felix himself! (Very distantly!) Herzliebe gruben aus Deutschland!
Your Maisie'

Postcard from Maisie to Gerard and Emily

*

Liverpool – 1 November 1938

Sam and Gerard were having lunch together.

'How is your father these days, Sam?'

Sam frowned. 'I'm not sure. He's very worried about young Maisie of course, as we all are. Have you heard from her lately?'

Gerard shook his head. 'She should be back any day, but we've heard nothing since the middle of last month.'

'I think my father is beginning to feel his age. Not that he'll admit it.'

'Sorry to hear that. At least you can give him one piece of good news. Tell him that I've talked about his case with the police council and they have assured me that whenever war is declared, he will automatically be classified as a Category C, friendly alien. So at least that's something he doesn't have to worry about.'

The waiter came over and Gerard asked for a 1920's claret. 'I know you aren't too fond of champagne, Sam. I think you'll enjoy this rather more.' He looked up at the waiter. 'And we'll both have some roast beef, as rare as possible. Does that sound all right Sam?'

'It sounds wonderful, thanks.'

As the waiter left, Sam said, 'We have all been horrified by the terrible news reports, but you must be as relieved as we are now by Chamberlain's recent announcement?'

Gerard looked grave, 'I might be – if I believed a word of it. War is inevitable, whatever that poor deluded man says. Germany hasn't managed to oust the Chancellor and that would be the only way to prevent it. My only hope is that as it hasn't started *yet*, my daft daughter should be safely home before all hell breaks loose. But I'm afraid it's only a matter of time. And that's the other reason why I wanted to see you today, Sam. Do you know anything about the Manchester Company, Arrow Aircraft?'

Sam nodded absently, 'yes, my brother Freddy ...' still appalled by what Gerard had just said.

Gerard went on, 'It's a subsidiary of Hawker Siddeley, and was originally started by Elliott Rowland, an old friend of mine. They were terrifically successful, designing brilliant new lightweight aircraft. But the depression has meant they've had to lay off a lot of men. Only now there is suddenly a huge demand for aviation and the original design company is back in business, taking orders from the RAF. This Government at least understands that air power will be vital in the event of war. Arrow are already working on designs for several new kinds of combat aircraft, and with Hawker Siddeley backing them, the sky's the limit – literally. I have already recommended that Eddie should go and see them and I believe young Freddy is already working for them.'

'Yes, I know. He told me.'

'Well, Sam. I happen to know that they are also looking for a new senior accountant, and I have told them all about you.'

'What do you mean, Gerard? I can't leave my firm!'

'Elliott wants to meet you. And Sam, I think it's time for you to consider leaving the security of the profession and to start working in developing industry. That's where your future lies, Sam, investing your own time and talent into helping new companies build up their business and becoming part of the process yourself.'

'Goodness me, Gerard, I'm nowhere near ready for a move like that. I've only been qualified for a little over a year. And I've got a wife to think about – we have a child on the way. Another problem is, Hazel wants her mother to move out of the big farmhouse she lives in now there's only Jenny still at home, so they may have to come and live with us for awhile.'

'Congratulations. I only wish my child were on her way ...' Gerard sighed and Sam was shocked to see a flash of agony pass over his face. Then Gerard shook his head and went on, 'Just come along and meet Elliott Rowland, Sam. Let's see if he can persuade you to let go a little of your security blanket. Life's no fun unless you take a few risks!'

*

The last postcard Gerard and Emily received from Maisie arrived in late October, saying she was on her way to Berlin to see Hans and the family, and that she would be home in two weeks. An earlier postcard had said that things were getting a bit tense in Hamburg and she was looking forward to coming home, but felt she must keep her promise to visit Hans and the family in Berlin first.

Now it was nearly the end of November, and they had heard nothing more from Maisie. Gerard sent a cable to Hans, who replied to say that Maisie had not arrived in Berlin. They had assumed she must have gone straight home.

Emily went into Gerard's study and found him sitting hunched over his desk, tapping and scowling ferociously. He shook his head at her when she came in. 'I knew I should have gone and brought her straight home. I just don't know what to do now. Damn the girl!'

'Maisie is very sensible, Gerard. I'm sure she will be all right. Hans will make sure she gets safely back.'

'Oh God! Emily, I can't just sit here. Something terrible must have happened. I have to find her.'

Liverpool – January 1939

Gerard returned home from Hamburg after a month, having found no trace of Maisie. There had been a violent pogrom against the Jews at the beginning of November, and Jewish businesses in Hamburg had all been ransacked. The city was now in a state of watchful siege. He managed to discover that the Mendelssohn family had disappeared just before what was now being called *Kristallnacht,* and none of their neighbours knew where they had gone. Someone thought they might be trying to make their way to England. Gerard persuaded a friend of the family to let him into the house to search, but there was no sign of either Maisie or her luggage or any message about where she might be.

Gerard caught the train to Berlin to see if she had arrived there. They still hadn't seen or heard from her. Hans told Gerard about what had just taken place in Berlin, with the destruction of Jewish property and synagogues, and he said that many of their own friends had disappeared, like the Mendelssohn family. He assured Gerard they would send him word the minute they had any news. Gerard spent a miserable Christmas in Berlin with Hans and Shirley and their two daughters.

Now he had to come home. From the middle of the 1930s, Britain immigration rules had suddenly become anti 'refuJews' and the ports were turning away all asylum seekers; but for now there was an amnesty on compassionate grounds after the horrors of *Kristallnacht* had become known.

All the boats and trains out of Germany were crowded with families making a last minute escape with as many of their possessions as they could manage. Nobody knew how long the amnesty would last. On the ferry they all told Gerard the same story, that they thought this was their last chance to escape. There were horror stories of other families trying to escape to Denmark in small boats that had ended up being drowned in the North Sea.

Emily went meet Gerard at the station and he nearly collapsed into her arms when he saw her.

'Oh God! Emily! Those bastards! I am so afraid that we now have to depend on the ridiculously small hope that she has gone into hiding with the Mendelssohns and by some miracle is still safe. Oh God! Oh God!'

18

History Repeats Itself

Manchester – September 1939

War was declared on 3 September.

William was confident that he would be classified as 'C', a 'friendly alien', and had registered promptly at the local police station, where they confirmed this, insisting only that he must keep them informed if he was planning to travel anywhere.

*

Liverpool – 4 September 1939

Gerard had written and telegrammed to everybody he had ever had any contact with in Germany. Nobody could give him any news of his daughter. 'Damn William! Why did he encourage her to go? I know what it is, Emily. The silly girl somehow feels responsible for the blasted Mendelssohn family and is trying to help them. We can only pray they are all safely hidden away somewhere. If only they'd get themselves out of Germany so she could come home. If only I could at least know that she is still alive.'

'Try and keep calm, dear. I'm sure we will hear from her soon.'

'Are you? I wish I were.'

Enemy Aliens

Manchester – June 1940

In the spring of 1940, the Germans overran the Low Countries and northern France in a shocking six-week *Blitzkrieg*, allegedly helped by an internal 'fifth column'. The British press once again began insisting on a round-up of all 'enemy aliens'.

In June, William, who over the past few months had been beginning to feel unwell for the first time in years, was once again taken into custody. He was sent first to a camp at an old disused mill at Huyton, and then a month later back to the Isle of Man. Eight-hundred-and-twenty-three men, all from Liverpool, nearly all of whom, apart from William, were aged 25 to 40, were taken across on the *Princess Josephine Charlotte*, a Belgium Cross Channel Vessel, and landed at Douglas.

It took them over an hour to disembark, each prisoner carrying a gasmask, watched by a silent, angry crowd held back by the police. No-one on the island had yet been issued with gasmasks.

The officer in charge on the shore said, 'Can anyone speak English?'

'Yes,' 800 men replied, in a variety of English accents.

They were marched over the Swing Bridge, with the officer in charge continually saying, 'Keep going.'

Gerard Belringer went with Leah, Albert, Edgar and Leo to see David Maxwell Fyfe, their member of parliament, to protest against William's incarceration.

'He is the father of seven British sons, all of whom are helping the war effort. How can anyone think their father is an enemy alien? We are all beside ourselves with worry. There is no question of him being any kind of alien, let alone an enemy. He loves this country. He came over as babe in arms – he knows nothing about Germany...' Leah stopped to draw breath and Maxwell Fyfe held up his hand to silence her.

'Believe me, madam, I completely understand. I give you my word I will use all my influence to get your husband released, Mrs, um, Logan. I'm sure you agree that when the security of the nation is at stake, it is better to be over-zealous rather than too liberal?' He glanced at Gerard. 'Gerard has given me the details about where your husband is being held. But you really must forgive me now – I have so many people to see. Good day to you.'

Leah and her sons continued to besiege David Maxell Fyfe with letters and Gerard advised them to get the family doctor to write as well. 'William has always refused to see Dr Ainsworth,' Leah said. 'He probably wouldn't know what he could say.'

Isle of Man – July 1940

This time there was no camp in the west. They were taken instead to the holiday resort towns of Ramsey and Douglas. Isle of Man residents complained bitterly in their local newspapers that they were being deprived of their livelihood now that so many holiday hotels and boarding houses along the sea-front promenade had been requisitioned and were surrounded by barbed wire to make a POW settlement for *'fascists, Mosleyites, and German spies.'*

William was held in one of a row of Victorian seaside bed and breakfast houses in Ramsey. The houses had all been stripped of soft furnishings, and the wooden stairs echoed noisily as the prisoners clattered up and down in their heavy boots. There were no curtains at the windows, sounds bounced off the cold plaster walls, and the floors were covered in worn brown linoleum, but the tall Victorian house couldn't quite lose its atmosphere as a place where people came to enjoy their holidays.

There were twelve German nationals in the same boarding house as William; four of them were Jewish refugees who had seen the way things were going in Berlin by the mid-1930s and had only just managed to sell up in time to escape to England. William shared a room with Julius Schmitt, a doctor who had arrived in Britain during the amnesty of December 1938; a year and a half later, Julius and his fellow Jews found themselves imprisoned behind barbed wire as enemy aliens by their country of sanctuary. The irony of their situation was not lost on any of the Jewish internees, but none of them thought they had made the wrong decision in leaving Germany.

Julius was more concerned for William than for himself when he saw how he had to struggle to get up the stairs, and how often he was being sick. 'You are a sick man, Wilhelm. You should not be here,' he told him. William shook his head. Privately he put his weakened condition down to his feelings of guilt and anxiety about Maisie.

'Oh I don't think it can be anything very serious. I'm just finding it difficult to digest my food at the moment. Just the penalty of old age, Julius! I must try to have a more positive attitude.'

Julius nodded and said, 'I see. Well if the symptoms get any worse, you must tell me. I would very much like to give you a proper examination, William.'

'I'm sure you don't need to do that. But thank you, Julius. You are very kind. If I ever wanted to see a doctor, you would be the one I would go to.'

Over the next few weeks William's condition deteriorated rapidly. He couldn't work and he was frequently sick. One morning he said to Julius, 'I am afraid there is some blood when I ...'

'OK Wilhelm. You must let me examine you now. It's no good trying to put it off, or it will only get worse.'

'Perhaps it might be wise. I don't want to pass on any infection to anyone else.'

Julius examined William. When he had finished, he said, 'I am sorry, Wilhelm. But it is as I thought. You need urgent medical attention.'

'What is it, do you think?'

'I am sorry. But it is probably best that you know the worst. I am almost certain you have bowel cancer, Wilhelm. Without a biopsy I can't be absolutely sure, but we must report it to the authorities. They will have to let you go home.'

'Cancer? No. It can't be.'

'I am so very sorry. I have very little doubt, Wilhelm. I am an oncologist in Germany. It is my specialism.'

Manchester – 1940

In December, starting on the Sunday before Christmas and lasting two nights, thousands of high explosive and incendiary bombs dropped on the city, in what was later known as the 'Manchester Blitz'. The whole city seemed to be lit up in a gigantic firework display. The bombardment began again on 9

January 1941 and the civic centre, Royal Exchange Free Trade Hall and Manchester Cathedral were all badly damaged.

The strain badly affected Sam's brother, Leo. He was a gentle, artistic soul and when an incendiary bomb came through their garage roof, he immediately moved his family to a remote farm cottage with no electricity on the Yorkshire Moors. Hazel went to help Leo and Martha move house and stayed with them for a few days while they settled in, leaving her own now eighteen-month old son, Mark, with his grandmother, Muriel, now ensconced in her new home in Cheadle.

Sam drove up to join them at the weekend, and Leo took a romantically lit photograph of Hazel and Sam sitting together on the floor by the fire. For a few days they all enjoyed each other's company, and tried to forget about the war. The two families had become very close over the last few years, and when Leo and Martha's baby daughter was born a year later, they christened her Margaret Hazel.

Manchester – April 1941

William was released from internment the following April, thanks to the medical inspector at Ramsey who confirmed that William was suffering from bowel cancer. A few days after his 70th birthday, William returned home.

19

'Black Sheep'

Manchester – 1941

William's sons were all now working in reserved occupations. None of them had wanted to try to join up for fear of the discovery of their original German family name and background, but they had all volunteered as home guards in their own neighbourhoods. Sam was still working for his old accountancy firm, Thomson McLintoch, and, like his brothers, was out nearly every night, fire-watching.

Thanks to Edgar, most of them now had access to cars or motor bikes and Freddy had taught them to drive. Edgar's business was being used by the army to service military vehicles, while he and Freddy were working for Arrow, making Lancaster bombers. Clifford, who had been travelling in Europe until 1938, working for Gerard Belringer, was now living in London with a job as an accounts clerk.

Leo worked at the garrison at Catterick designing camouflage materials for tanks and ships. He was able to do most of his work from home, but whenever he needed to appear at Catterick, his wife, Martha would drive him there and wait for him outside in the car. He was nervous about driving, refused to answer the telephone, and lived in a constant state of high anxiety for the safety of his family.

William was too ill to go back to work in his bookshop and was unhappy that he could now do so little to support Leah, but he was able to continue working in the garden which supplied most of the food they needed. They even had a few chickens and rabbits in the orchard, and once again all the beds were turned over to growing vegetables, so that Leah could offer soup to her sons whenever they called round.

Since the beginning of the war, Leah had been doing a part time job at the local hospital preparing meals for the nursing staff. Once William was home, the family, mainly their daughters-in-law, took it in turns to sit with him on the afternoons Leah was out.

William walked slowly downstairs and inspected himself in the hall mirror. Leah was in the kitchen preparing his breakfast. He sat down heavily at the kitchen table as a spasm of pain overwhelmed him.

Fellow-prisoners on the Isle of Man had told him about things that were happening in Germany so vile and sickening that he did not want to believe them. Neither could he bear to think about what might have happened to his dear niece, Maisie. He knew that Gerard blamed him – nearly as much as he bitterly blamed himself. He was also convinced that all his sons were angry with him for the trouble his German nationality was still causing them all.

He looked at Leah, busy making his tea with boiling water from the huge iron kettle hanging over the range and said, 'I do know that I have become the black sheep of our family, Leah.' Leah shook her head. 'Oh Will! What a thing to say! Of course you are no such thing! We all love you.'

Blackburn – May 1943

In 1943 Sir John Nettles, who had been highly impressed by Sam when he had done his firm's audit, invited him to join his family-owned light aircraft company in Blackburn to work as joint Managing Director with his own son, Jack Nettles. The former MD and chief accountant had both been called up, and the Company had had no-one in charge for several months. Urged on by Hazel, Sam decided to accept.

The company's traditional industry was making sporting gliders, light aircraft and toy aeroplanes, but now they had government contracts to build dozens of large gliders and tow-ing planes for transporting troops across to France. When he had done the firm's audit, Sam had suggested to Sir John that he should perhaps be thinking about reducing or even closing down the part of the factory making leisure equipment for the duration of the war. Sam now realised that he was the one who would have to put this into effect.

Sam and Jack Nettles were both young men still in their twenties and neither of them had ever had to take on so much responsibility. They were both very reluctant to take the step of firing any men. After the first few weeks, they began to transfer as many as possible over to the war work, but that still left nearly fifty men who would have to be laid off.

When he realised that there was now no alternative if the company was to remain solvent, Sam didn't think he could face seeing the men one by one in his office. He decided instead to summon the whole company to the works canteen and explain the situation to them all over a loud hailer.

There was immediate uproar and an all-out strike was called. In spite of Sir John defending Sam's action and pleading for him to have a second chance, the Board of Directors passed a vote of no confidence in Sam, who was dismissed.

Two days later, a shocked Sam returned home. Gerard met his train and told him, 'Whatever you do, don't say anything to the press.'

When a journalist from the *Daily Express* arrived at the house to speak to him, Sam said, 'I have nothing to say' and closed the door. The man kept banging on the door until Sam opened it again in a rage; the next day there was a picture of a furious-looking Sam shaking his fist. The caption read: 'Sacked Managing Director at home in his Marple residence.'

Realising that Sam was on the point of nervous collapse, Hazel made him go to see their doctor, who prescribed a month's seclusion and rest at a sanatorium by the sea at Bridlington. Sam was too dazed and unhappy to argue. He watched helplessly as Hazel packed his suitcase, took him to the station in a taxi and put him on the train.

He took long walks by the sea. After a week, Sam slowly began to pull himself together. To avoid thinking round and round about what had happened, he began trying to remember everything Leo had taught him about colour. He brought himself some water-colour paints and challenged himself to produce seascapes without using the colour blue.

He came home before the end of the month, and sat down to write letters applying for work. He grew used to receiving rejection letters or, in many cases, no response at all. Even his old firm, Thomson McLintoch, regretted that they had no vacancy. When Hazel tried to talk to him about Mark, who was now nearly four, Sam looked at her in surprise for a moment, then went back to writing letters.

After four months, he received one positive reply. It came from Crichton and Borthwick, a firm of accountants in London. Sam nearly fainted with relief.

Hazel said, 'Would that mean we would have to move to London? You know how much Mother needs me here, with Jenny so poorly ...'

'Let's just see if they offer me a job first, before we worry about that. In any case, I would go down on my own at first, and live in digs. But let's just wait and see. If they offer me anything, I will have to accept. I have to work, Pet.'

In spite of the disaster in Blackburn, Sam had been given good references by his old boss at Thomson McLintoch, as well as by Sir John Nettles and Gerard Belringer, who all wrote letters to Sir Charles Crichton to support his application. Sir Charles conducted the interview himself in his private office.

'I hear some good things of you, Mr Logan.'

'Thank you, Sir.'

'So tell me, how do you see the role of the accountant in modern business, Mr Logan?'

'Well, Sir. I believe the real business of our country lies in innovation and manufacturing – inventing and making things – and we have many brilliant engineers and innovators. But I also believe that good accountancy has its own major part to play. I always say that a good manufacturing idea will always work out well at the end of my pencil.'

'Otherwise?'

'Otherwise? Oh – otherwise it isn't a good idea!'

Sir Charles laughed and nodded. 'And what do you think the main reasons are for a good idea *not* to work out well at the end of your pencil, Mr Logan?'

'Well, Sir, if the books are properly balanced and there are good relations between management and the shop floor, things will always go well. Problems arise when a successful enter-prise stops taking care about balancing the true costs of new ideas against the likely rewards. In other words, stops paying attention to the logic of my pencil. Then too much is spent re-warding the directors and managers with company cars and expense account lunches and there is a failure to acknowledge the requirements of the workforce. Then they are surprised when the money quickly drains away.'

Sir Charles said, 'Talking of the requirements of the shop floor – Mr Logan, I know all about what happened at Black-burn. It was very unfortunate. Sir John is a good friend and has told me the whole story. I believe that it can be put down to a misjudgement of youth, and I hope you have learned a valuable lesson. What you have said to me today makes a lot of sense. I will have to talk to my Board to get their agreement, of course, before I can promise anything, but you have made a good first impression on me and you have excellent references, so I think I can at least offer you some hope for a good outcome.'

Sam stood up. 'Thank you very much, Sir. I can assure you that if you give me this opportunity, I will work hard and do everything in my power to justify your faith in me.'

Sir Charles stood up too and shook Sam's hand. 'I'm sure you will. Thank you very much for coming to see me, Mr Logan. If you would call in on my secretary on your way out, she will reimburse your travelling expenses from Manchester. You will be hearing from us one way or the other very soon.'

Manchester – September 1943

Sam accepted the post he was offered as a senior auditor with Crichton and Borthwick.

Hazel had discovered that she was pregnant. When she had been expecting Mark, she had never felt better, but this time she was feeling very sick and listless and wanted to have her mother nearby. She was also becoming increasingly worried about Muriel. 'I think Mother thinks she is dying, Sam. She keeps asking what will happen to Jenny when she's gone. She really needs me here.' Sam decided that they should sell their house in Marple, and that Hazel and Mark should stay with Muriel in her new home in Cheadle, while he rented a room in

South London with the family of one of his new firm's directors.

He could only manage to travel home for the occasional weekend, sometimes coming back through the night on the troop trains, but one Friday evening he was able leave work in the morning and telephoned to say he would be back in Manchester by 6 p.m.

Hazel wanted to meet him off the train so that they could have their high tea together in town and then go to see a film – something that was becoming an extremely rare treat. She had arranged to sit with Sam's father, William, that afternoon, so she said to her mother. 'Will you will be all right if I leave you alone with Mark this afternoon and then all evening, Mother? I'm sitting with Father-in-law after lunch and then I want to meet Sam off the train so we can see a film before coming home.'

Muriel picked Mark up. 'There is nothing I would like better. We'll have lots of fun on our own, won't we, Mark?' Mark reached up and touched her head and nodded seriously. His mother and grandmother laughed fondly.

'You are sure it won't be too much for you?'

'I'll be fine – we'll go for a walk and then we'll both probably have a little nap this afternoon, won't we, Little Man?'

*

Leah greeted Hazel at the door.

'William will be so pleased to see you. I don't know what we'd do without all you kind girls. Go straight in. He is awake'

Hazel wandered into the sitting room where William was lying on the couch, covered in a blanket, reading.

'What a beautiful surprise!' he said when he saw her. He began to try to get up, but she quickly sat down on the chair beside him and looked at the cover of his book.

'*One Pair of Feet.* Is it any good?'

'I brought it for Leah, but I'm enjoying it myself. Monica Dickens. She is the great-granddaughter of Charles Dickens, Sam's great hero!'

'And mine!'

'And mine. This is her second book and I think she is very talented. She is also a very charming young lady. I met her when she came into my office when we had just published her first book.'

'Is she another of your many young lady correspondents, Father-in-law?'

William laughed. 'Leah thinks I am far too interested in my young lady writers! But I like to encourage all young writers, not only young females.'

'Perhaps Mother-in-law will lend me this when you've finished it?'

'Of course, my dear.'

Leah looked round the door. 'I'm off now, William. Can I get you anything before I go?'

He beamed at her. 'No, no, I don't think so. Just having this lovely young lady here is already making me feel better.' He took Hazel's hand for a moment and gave it a little shake.

'Well, if the pain starts, you must tell Hazel straight away, so she can give you your medicine.'

'Yes, of course.'

'Well, goodbye then.'

'Goodbye, my dear.'

'I shall be home by five.'

Leah smiled at Hazel, gave William one last anxious glance, and left the house.

'Now tell me, my dear, is there any news of your young brother in Singapore?'

'No. We have heard nothing from Alan since the Christmas before last. I am afraid it is making my mother ill with worry. And the longer the war goes on, of course, the worse things seem to get.'

'I hope she is managing to keep her spirits up. Please tell her how much we think about her. Having you and Mark with her must be a blessing. How is my grandson? And how are you? How long is it before the baby arrives?'

'Oh a long time yet. And Mark is fine – he loves all his grandparents and is thoroughly spoiled by my mother. Now – are you quite sure you are warm enough?'

'Quite warm, thank you. I shall probably fall asleep. I hope you won't think me rude. I usually take a nap in the afternoons these days.'

'That's a good idea. I'll just sit over here and look at the garden.' Hazel got up and went to sit in a chair by the window so she could look out into the garden. After a few minutes she said, 'Your garden is still looking beautiful. I love the autumn colours.'

He didn't answer, and after a moment she turned round and saw that he had fallen asleep, the book still in his hands. She got up and went over to retrieve it, and sat down again by the window to read it herself. The afternoon ticked by. William groaned a little in his sleep, but didn't wake up.

At quarter past five Hazel looked at her watch and stood up. Leah had said she would be home by five. She went outside to see if she could see her coming up the road. She went back in and sat down again and waited for another five minutes. If she didn't leave soon, she'd be too late to meet Sam at the station. She straightened up William's blanket, and looked at him, but he didn't wake up. He seemed to be in a deep sleep.

'I'll be off now, Father Will,' she said softly to him. 'Mother-in-law will be home very soon.' And she crept out of the room, and out of the house, and walked down the road to the tram.

When Leah got home twenty-minutes later she found William alone in the house, screaming in agony. He had been sick and had had a violent attack of diarrhoea.

'I'm sorry!' William gasped. 'I'm so sorry to be such a trouble.'

Leah held him, weeping. Then she gave him his tablets, although the pain was now too great for them to make much difference. Then she helped him through to the kitchen and washed him down, and put him to bed. Eventually William fell asleep.

There was a dreadful quarrel. Leah was incandescent with fury, but Hazel refused to accept that she was to blame. She kept saying to Sam and her own mother, 'Mother-in-law said she'd be home by five. I didn't leave until nearly half-past. He was peacefully asleep when I left. I thought she'd be back at any moment.'

Sam stood up for his wife.

'Mother, you know that Hazel would never have knowingly let Father come to any harm. She loves him. How could she possibly know that he would suddenly have such a dreadful attack? It was a terrible thing to happen, but surely you can see that it wasn't Hazel's fault.'

'We shall not be asking her to help us again,' Leah replied coldly.

London – February 1944

A loud crash made Clifford suddenly freeze, thinking it was a flying bomb. It was nearly midnight. Then he realised it was someone banging loudly at the door. Because of the blackout the small hallway of the flat was in darkness apart from the narrow strip of light emerging through the sitting room door from the lamp on the desk where he had been working. He opened the front door cautiously. Two tall, serious-looking men were standing outside. One of the men was in uniform, the other in plain clothes, but they were both clearly policemen.

'Can I help you?'

Cold air blew in.

'Mr Logan? Mr Clifford Logan?'

'That is my name. How can I help you?'

'We must ask you to come along with us to the Police Station, Sir. There are one or two questions we need to ask you.'

'Questions? What sort of questions?'

'Down at the Station, Sir, the matter will be explained to you there.'

'Do you have a warrant?'

'That won't be necessary at the moment, Sir. We just need you to help us with our enquiries by answering a few questions. Do you have a coat?'

'In the middle of the night? This is absolutely outrageous.'

Clifford marched back into the living room, picked up his jacket from the back of his sofa where he had slung it, turned off the lamp, took an overcoat from the hall and followed them out of the flat locking his front door behind him. They led the way down the cold, dark stairwell of the Edwardian block of flats and out into the street, where a police car was waiting. The driver was standing on the pavement stamping his feet and chaffing his arms. He jumped to attention when he saw them and opened the doors of the black Rover to let them in. The plain clothes man sat in the front with the driver, and the uniformed officer, a huge man with a black moustache, sat silently next to Clifford on the back seat.

The car sped off through the dark, deserted London streets. The driver braked to avoid a line of ducks waddling calmly across the Strand. At the next junction Clifford had a glimpse of a fox disappearing down an alley.

Inside the police station, the uniformed officer spoke to a sergeant at the desk who let them through into a large office at the back.

'Can I get you a cup of tea, Sir?'

'Thank you.'

The uniformed policeman went to the door and called out into the corridor, 'Bring us in some tea please, Sergeant.'

His colleague was studying a piece of paper on the table in front of him. When the Inspector came back and sat down, the other man looked up and said to Clifford,

'Your full name is Clifford Morgan Logan?

'That is correct.'

'You are currently employed by C. Lilley Ltd?'

'Yes...?'

'And you began employment with them just over three years ago?'

'Yes. About then. Look here, I wish you would tell me what this is all about.'

'And prior to that you were travelling abroad?'

'Yes. I was based in Brussels and travelling to and from Switzerland. I was acting on behalf of a previous employer.'

'Your previous employer was?'

'I was acting on behalf of Mr Gerard Belringer. Mr Belringer is my uncle by marriage.'

'And at that time, was your name Clifford Logan?'

'Yes .Of course it was. That is my name.'

'Have you by any chance had any reason to change your name since you left Mr Belringer's employment?'

'No! Why should I? Whatever do you mean?'

'We have a document here, signed by you, C. Lohmann.'

'I expect it is just my appalling handwriting – if it *is* something I signed. Can I see this document?'

'And you have no connection with anyone of the name of Lohmann?'

So this was what this was all about. The bloody name.

'Is that why you have brought me here in the middle of the night? Because of my name? Well. Yes. I confess. I may have used the wrong name by mistake. My father happens to have a German name and for what must be obvious reasons even to you, we decided to change the family name to Logan some years ago. However, I can assure you that I am a true Englishman born and bred. My brother, Samuel Logan, is a highly respected member of his profession and I'm sure he will vouch for me. '

'Your father is a German, and you used the German form of your name on this occasion? Would you like to tell me why?'

'I honestly *can't* tell you. By mistake, I suppose. And my father is only technically of German descent – he came to this country as a small child and has lived here ever since. He is as English as you or I. Look here, are you going to tell me what this is all about?'

'Until April 1941, your father was interned on the Isle of Man as an enemy alien, was he not?'

'Yes indeed he was. It was a cruel mistake that was corrected by the intervention of our member of parliament. My family have since had a full apology. He is now at home, a very sick man.'

'Can you tell me the reason why you left your last employer?'

'I couldn't continue to act as Gerard Belringer's agent once the war made travelling abroad impossible. Also, I wanted to be based in England to be of help to my mother, particularly when my father was unjustly interned. I came back solely because of the war.'

'Would you be surprised to know that it has come to light that somebody in your present company has for a longish period been converting capital into foreign currency?'

'Well, all companies do that. Money gets transferred into overseas accounts. We do a lot of our business with overseas clients. It is normal.'

'This would be your own department, Sir? You work in the department for overseas development?'

'Yes. I am a clerk within that department.'

'So you would have noticed any unusual transactions.'

It was not a question.

'My brother, Samuel, audited our accounts – he will vouch for me. I knew nothing about any unusual transactions of the kind you describe. I wish to speak to my solicitor unless this interview stops now. I don't understand at all why I am here. There are many more senior men than I am who should be answering your questions. I seem to have been made a scapegoat.'

Two days previously Sam had received a late-night telephone call from Gerard Belringer, warning him that Clifford seemed to have got himself into some serious trouble.

'Oh no! Don't tell me. He wasn't involved with this business at Lily's was he?'

'It looks like it I'm afraid. How did you know about that?'

'I began their audit last year and discovered some discrepancies in the overseas accounts. I reported that I suspected that some fraudulent conversion of funds into foreign currency might be going on. A colleague of mine did the follow up, and he confirmed my suspicions, and reported it to their Management Board. I was working on another account by then and didn't hear any more about it. Someone at Lily's must have passed it on to the police. But surely Clifford isn't in a position to pull off a thing like that? He's just a junior accounts clerk...'

'... in the department for overseas development, from where money is routinely converted into foreign currency. Precisely. The police have been round here all day asking me questions. It seems Clifford has been using some of the contacts he made when he was working for me in Brussels to transfer funds from Lily's to an account in Switzerland. A large sum of money – nearly five hundred pounds – can't be accounted for. They don't know how the trick was done, but they may have traced it back to Clifford. You need to cover your own back, Sam. You don't want your name to be associated with his if you can help it.'

Clifford was allowed home that night, and ordered to report back to the police station the following morning. The next day he was charged with embezzlement and held in police custody. Sam had not mentioned to his own employers the fact that his brother was employed at C. Lily when he had originally been sent to do their audit, and he took Gerard's advice and made no mention of it now. He reasoned that Logan was a common enough name and there was no reason why anyone should assume there was a family connection. When the police contacted him he said the audit at Lily's had been done by a colleague, and he himself had not been aware that his brother was working there.

*

'Samuel! He is your brother…. Why could you not have helped him? Do you want to utterly destroy me?'

Leah had telephoned Sam as soon as she had heard from Gerard that Clifford had been arrested.

'Mother, Clifford is a thief. I had no idea that he was involved in all this, but no good would come from my trying to speak up for him now, and a lot of harm could come to me. I could lose my job if I had failed to report a malfeasance or tried to cover it up. And Clifford would still be Clifford. You would have two sons ruined.'

'You should have done something. You should have talked to him, warned him, given him time to put things right, not reported him like some common criminal. Now what is to become of him?'

'Clifford always lands on his feet, Mother. I expect he'll manage to get himself out of this mess one way or another. I only know that he isn't doing it at my expense.'

'Oh yes, we all know that. Nothing must ever be done to inconvenience you, Samuel. You and Hazel both seem to think you are too good for the rest of us. Well you are not too good.

You and Hazel are the black sheep of this family, not my poor, misguided Clifford.'

*

Manchester – March 1944

William went back into hospital in the middle of March where they managed to help control the pain. After two weeks they sent him home, but he and Leah both knew now that he was coming home to die.

'I am not afraid, Leah. My faith in the Goodness that is in charge of us all has come back more strongly than ever. God is working for us. All will be well, because there is truth and love and hope in our family.'

'Not in all our family,' Leah said sadly.

'All,' William insisted. 'We mustn't let misunderstandings lead to harsh judgement. I know that the reason our family will remain together and always be a strong unit is because you yourself are strong. I don't know, dearest Leah, how I could ever have come to such feelings of peace and hope if it had not been for all the love and strength you have always shown.'

20

Heimat

Manchester – April 1944

Sam was in his office in London when he received the news that his father had died. Although, in spite of his brother Freddy's teaching, he was still an inexperienced driver, he asked to borrow a company car to make the journey home for the funeral.

Arriving in Cheadle late that night, he was greeted by Muriel, who warned him that Hazel was not feeling at all well and had gone to bed. He went up to her room and saw that she was looking very pale and gaunt, but she smiled when she saw him. 'Hello, Sam. I'm sorry I couldn't wait up but I seem to be having rather a lot of trouble this time. Have you had anything to eat yet?'

'Not yet. Your mother is boiling me an egg. I'm worried about you, Pet. Have you seen the doctor?'

'Yes. He just says it is the baby making his presence felt. At least it's not too long to go now. I think it's the miserable rations we're living on that have upset us both. Mother isn't well either. I do hope you've remembered to bring your book with you?'

'Of course! I've given it to Muriel, and I had purloined some of the office tea supply, so she's very pleased. Well, you go back to sleep now. I'll go downstairs and leave you in peace.'

Downstairs, Muriel told Sam how Hazel could no longer face coming out to the shelter when the sirens sounded and preferred sit under the kitchen table with Mark. 'She's not at all her old self, I'm afraid.'

'Thank you for looking after them both. I don't know what we'd do without you.'

'Oh Hazel will soon be well again once the baby is born. It's my poor Jenny I worry about more.'

Sam drove Mark into Manchester for William's funeral, which was being held in the family home. The Christian Science teacher who had become a good friend of William's would be conducting a short service. Leah swept Mark up in her arms as soon as they arrived saying, 'Hello, my young stranger!' When she put him down Mark ran into the kitchen to find the old dog, Juno.

Leah turned to Sam, 'You managed to get here then.'

'Of course I came, Mother.'

'Well – I'm glad you are here. Come through and see. We have a surprise visitor.' She led him through into the sitting room where his brothers and their wives had gathered. Gerard and Emily were talking seriously to another man with his back to the door, who had his arm around Emily's shoulders. As Sam went over to greet them, the man turned round and said, 'Now don't tell me – see if I can remember. You must be ... Sam! Is that right? But my! How you've grown since I last you!'

Gerard said, 'Yes, it's surprising how much a young boy will grow in twenty years, Freddie!'

'Uncle Freddie!' Sam looked amazed as he shook hands with his uncle. 'How are you? It's very good to see you after all this time.'

Freddie looked serious. 'I know it's been too long. But Kent is a long way from Manchester. I've just been asking after our Maisie, and Gerard and Emily have told me the dreadful news.' He turned back to Gerard.

'You mustn't give up hope. There is a good chance she's being kept safe somewhere. There are still many good people living in Germany.'

'I've never given up hope,' Gerard said firmly. 'It's just so frustrating that I can't go over there and bring her back.'

'My shop has taken a direct hit, I'm afraid. A bomb landed smack bang in the middle. We've lost everything. There's nothing left.'

'What will you do now?'

'My wife's people all live in Chester so we'll be moving up there. So at least I'll be nearer here if I can be of any help to Leah. I have been away from you all far too long.'

Cheadle – May 3, 1944

'My breathing is getting worse. Dr says it's a fever and must stay in bed. Hazel still poorly.'

Muriel's diary

Hazel woke up in great pain in the middle of the night. She called out and Muriel came in to her room with a candle, 'What is it, dear?'

Hazel groaned and clutched her stomach. She was lying curled up in a ball. Muriel pulled back the blankets and could see that Hazel's nightdress and sheets were soaked with blood. She covered her daughter up again. 'Hold on, darling. I think I had better call the doctor.' When she came back from the telephone she sat down on the bed and held her daughter's hand. 'He won't be long. I must just go and boil the kettle.'

'Has the baby started?'

'Yes. I think so.'

The doctor arrived quarter of an hour later with his wife, a trained midwife, and between them over the next four hours they helped Hazel give birth to a little boy. The tiny baby was washed and wrapped in a towel. After a moment's hesitation the doctor handed him to Hazel who was holding out her arms. She held the baby, kissed him gently and looked up tearfully at her mother before handing him back to the doctor. The little boy looked perfect, but he had been still-born.

For a few more days, Hazel stayed in bed. Then one morning she got up early and went downstairs to the kitchen. Muriel smiled and hugged her when she appeared, and Mark shouted 'Mummy!' and got down from the table and ran over and hugged her legs. She picked him up. 'Oh how I've missed my boy. Have you been good while Mummy has been poorly?'

'He has. He's been Granny's little angel, haven't you Mark?'

Mark nodded gravely. 'We've been writing letters to Daddy, and to all his uncles, haven't we Mark. We think Uncle Tom is coming home on leave next week.'

'Still no news from Alan?'

'No. But I truly believe that he's alive. I'm sure I would know if he weren't.'

Hazel sat down with Mark on her lap. 'Could I have a cup of tea, do you think? Have we got any tea?'

'Yes, I've saved a little from Sam's last visit. I'll make us both a pot. Are you beginning to feel a little stronger now, dear?'

'I'm all right. I still don't seem to have much energy.'

'When you've got your strength back, I think it is time for you to go down to London to be with Sam. Mark will hardly remember his father he has seen so little of him.'

'I don't want to leave you on your own, Mother ....'

'Nonsense. I have Jimmy, and all my sisters and your cousin, Nancy, who all rally round. I will miss you, of course, we all will, but you and Mark need to be with Sam now. And he needs you. Your place is with him. You will still all come and visit me sometimes, I should hope!'

'Well – we will go – but not yet.'

Cheadle, August 7, 1944

'Still very tired. Jimmy came with some eggs. He visited Jenny for me this pm. Letter from Tom, now in Egypt.'

Muriel's diary

August 13

'Hazel down to London to see flat Sam has found.'

Muriel's diary

Hazel was depressed and ill for a long time after losing the baby, but having travelled down to London on the train that August to look at the two bed-roomed flat that Sam thought they could afford in South West London, she began to feel ready to make the move. The art-deco block of flats was on a hill and looked across the road to Richmond Park. Her only anxiety was for her mother, because although Muriel was urging her to join Sam, Hazel knew that Muriel was not well herself, and that Jenny's worsening epilepsy and still having no news of Alan was breaking her heart.

October 29

'S. brought car round at 10.30 to take Hazel and Mark down to London. Shall feel very lost without them.'

Muriel's diary

After a tearful farewell with her Mother, Hazel got in beside Sam in his borrowed company car, a big Daimler of which he was inordinately proud. Mark sat on her lap to begin with, then climbed over onto the back seat.

Once they were out of town, Sam began to drive fast, excited by the car's power. He was about to overtake the car in front, when that driver swerved out into the middle of the road in front of him to avoid some debris. Sam slammed on his brakes and blasted on his horn, swearing loudly. Hazel leaned over to the back and reached out to stop Mark from being hurled onto the floor. 'For God's sake! Do be more careful, Sam!'

'It's that bloody idiot! He shouldn't be allowed on the road.' The car in front pulled back to the left and Sam overtook, shaking his fist and scowling at the other driver as they passed. 'You shouldn't drive so close to other cars.'

Sam wound down his window and spat out of it before closing it up again. 'You saw that! The bloody fool swerved out in front of me.'

'Well please calm down now.'

'Was it another Bloody Road Hog, Daddy?' came a cheerful voice from the back.

Sam laughed, 'It was another Bloody Road Hog, Mark! Mummy doesn't understand the right terminology.'

Hazel raised her eyes to heaven. After a while, Sam began to sing '*Old Man River*' in his deep bass voice and Mark joined in. Hazel found to her surprise that she was beginning to feel almost happy.

'Sam ...?'

'Yes, dear?'

'We're going to have another ...'

Sam began to break suddenly with surprise, then looked in his mirror just in time to accelerate and avoid the car behind colliding into him. The driver hooted angrily and overtook them, shaking his fist. Hazel laughed, 'Now you know what you look like!'

'But – are you quite sure? Isn't it a bit soon ...?'

'I feel fine, Sam. It's only just started, but I know it's going to be all right this time. It feels quite different. It felt wrong all along last time.'

Sam looked in his driving mirror at his son, sitting watching them from the back seat. 'Better not say anything yet.'

'No. But it's going to be fine. I'm sure it is.'

Sam said to Mark, 'We're all going to live together in our very own home, Mark. Will you like that?'

'Can we have a dog?'

'Why not? I've missed having a dog too.'

'What will we call him, Mark?'

'Rumpelstilzchen. It's my favourite Grandpa story.'

*

Richmond – April 1945

'I think you should come home quickly,' it was Hazel's brother, Tom on the telephone. 'It's mother,'

'Is she ...?'

'Yes. I'm afraid so. She wants to see you.'

Hazel telephoned Sam at work. 'I'm going to get a train home. Tom thinks Mother is dying. Elsie will come to look after Mark, but can you get home early?'

Sitting alone on the train to Manchester, Hazel, now heavily pregnant, felt very tense and anxious. She tried to read a magazine, but couldn't concentrate. At last she dozed off. An hour later she woke up suddenly with an overwhelming feeling of peace.

Tom met her at the station. As soon as she saw his face, she knew. 'I'm so sorry, Hazel ... I am afraid you are too late.'

'I know.'

*

Berlin – 1945

As soon as the war ended, Gerard Belringer managed to secure permission to travel to Germany as part of a delegation to look at the problems of the resettlement of displaced refugees. Berlin was in ruins, but Gerard scarcely noticed his surroundings. Working alongside the delegation by day, he spent his nights going through Nazi administration records searching for Maisie's name.

In the short time he was there he managed to scan hundreds of the German administration's meticulously kept lists of the names of all prisoners and their fates: executions, labour camps, experimentations, concentration camps, confiscations of property.

He had to return to England at the end of the first month but made arrangements to return to Berlin after the terms of peace had been settled between the allies. He had found no trace of Maisie on any list.

Berlin – January 1947

It was nearly two years before Gerard could return to Berlin to resume his search for Maisie. He couldn't keep hoping that she might still be alive somewhere, but he was determined never to give up until he knew what had become of her. He was able only with a lot of difficulty to get permission to travel to the Eastern sector now controlled by the Russians, where he believed the Schindler's lived in Invalidenstrasse.

Even though Gerard had visited Berlin on many occasions and knew it well, he was finding it nearly impossible to recognise his old landmarks. He could only wonder that anybody could have survived such total devastation. He walked through miles of ruined streets where tired men were at work clearing away the rubble brick by brick into trucks so they could reuse the material. New buildings were slowly going up, but thousands of people were still wandering around the city streets, appearing lost and homeless.

Eventually he found Hans and Shirley Schindler in a newly built concrete block of flats. Hans' widowed sister Margarethe and her youngest daughter were living with them. Hans and his son, both architects, were engaged in turning the rubble of the ruined city into utilitarian blocks of flats.

Hans told Gerard about the horrific last weeks of the war in the city. 'Before, with the allied bombings, although they were terrible, at least there was some advance warning, so we could get down into the cellar. But once the Russians came, it was different. By then we were all nearly starving. We were eating mice and rats. If you went out to find food, the artillery fire and shelling and bombing were random, there was no warning, and it was deadly. Shells would suddenly hit right into the crowds queuing for rations. And you maybe have already seen how they destroyed *Unter den Linden*, the *Kurfurstendamm*, and the *Tiergarten?* Everywhere you look you see it. If you went out after an attack you saw pieces of clothing and even human flesh hanging from the trees. People were given no time to take cover – they were just blown to bits. Even the *Stadstschloss* is in ruins – have you seen? But I assure you, we shall build it all again.'

Invalidenstrasse – 30 January

'The whole city has become a scene of indescribable carnage. The fanatical remnants of Hitler's supporters went on trying to defend it and save the Third Reich right up to the last minute and the Russians have exacted a terrible vengeance for the acts of barbarity and cruelty in the labour camps and concentration camps. Hans tells me that countless women and girls here have been raped by Russian soldiers, and men, women and children have been shot or buried under collapsing buildings.'

Letter from Gerard to Sam 1947

The older generation were all dead. Margarethe told Gerard that she was trying to get permission to move with her daughter either to the British or American sector because she was so terrified of the Russians, but Berliners trying to escape to West Berlin were being arrested.

'Perhaps you could help, Gerard? I am too old now to leave Germany, but my daughter.... And she has many friends. This is no place for young women. Could you perhaps help to get papers so they can travel to England?'

Gerard promised to do what he could and that he would come back soon. Neither Hans nor Margarethe could suggest what might have happened to Maisie. Along with thousands of others during those years, she had simply disappeared.

Hans told him that all things considered, he was in good heart. 'Things will get better, you will see. Berlin has always been a great city for architects. Whatever we build today, somebody will come along and pull down tomorrow, and then they have to employ another architect to design something to replace it! It is what we do here in Berlin.'

Gerard found only desolation.

21

A Family Reunion

Sussex – June 1964

They could all be heard laughing downstairs.

Alice and Mark's cousin, Margo, and her parents, Leo and Martha Logan, had driven down from Manchester the night before to stay for two days with Alice and Mark and their parents, Sam and Hazel. Margo's family were on their way to a holiday in France. Alice was meeting other members of her father's family for the first time. Even Mark hadn't seen them since he was a small child.

Alice was drawn to her uncle and aunt immediately – two warm, friendly people who had both given her a loving hug and seemed delighted to meet her. Unlike her own parents, Uncle Leo and Auntie Martha had soft, slightly northern voices which Alice found very attractive. Leo and Sam were clearly brothers, with the same banana smile and big brown eyes they had inherited from their father. Margo was a little more reserved than her parents, but she too seemed very pleased to meet her cousins. Now the grown-ups, including Mark, were talking and laughing in the sitting room while Alice and Margo were upstairs in Alice's bedroom.

Alice, skinny and tall in a stretchy black cat-suit was sitting cross-legged on the bed looking at an old notebook her cousin had brought for her to see. She stared at her cousin: 'So I had a great-aunt Alice!' Margo, a little shorter and plumper than her cousin, had light brown curly hair, but with brown eyes like Alice. She was wearing a smart tweed skirt and Jaeger sweater and was sitting slightly awkwardly on a small chair covered in Alice's discarded clothes. ('Don't worry – they all need ironing anyway.')

Margo smiled. 'Didn't your father ever tell you anything about our family history?'

'Not really. Hardly at all. Mum used to tell us lots of stories about her family, but Dad never really talks about his. He's certainly never said anything about being German – or even that he actually had an Aunt Alice!' She frowned at the next page of the diary. 'So – the family must have been ... Otto and Anna, and their children were Wilhelm, *Alice*, Emily and Freddie ... so Dad's brother Freddy was probably named after our *Great* Uncle Freddie? '

'I expect so. I met Great Uncle Freddie once.'

'Did you? Golly! What was he like? Did *he* seem German?'

'No. I don't think so. It was a long time ago. I can't remember much about him. He came over to see Grandmother one day when I was very young.

'What was she like – our grandmother?'

'She wasn't very easy to have living with you – especially if you were a girl. She thought boys were the only ones that mattered. My mother said she'd always been like that – all her daughters-in-law were scared of her!'

'Mum did tell me that too! And that she always had a hot meal ready in the oven in case any of her sons arrived home unexpectedly – long after they had all grown up and married and left home! Can you believe it?'

They both laughed disbelievingly.

Alice said, 'There is one thing Dad *has* told us about – how every Christmas Eve Grandfather Will would shut them all out of the living room while he spent the evening decorating the tree with silver baubles and hanging it with hundreds of little candles, and there was a little crib scene at the bottom. And then at midnight he would blow a bugle or a trumpet or something, and the boys would all run downstairs to see the tree and receive their presents.'

Margo was nodding in agreement. 'Yes – yes I know ... and if it was snowing, Grandfather Will would even go out and laid sledge tracks on the lawn!'

'Oh! How sweet! Poppa still always stays up late on Christmas Eve, playing the Messiah on some old 78s he's got while we all go off to midnight mass. He doesn't decorate the tree – Mark and I always do that – but when we come back, he is always waiting up for us to give us our presents. I'm always so tired by then – but Poppa won't wait until morning. He says it's a "family tradition", and when he was a boy they all sang *Silent Night* before they went to bed.'

'Yes – but it wasn't 'Silent Night' they sang – it was 'Stille Nacht' – in German.'

'Oh!'

The two girls looked at each other in silence. Then Margo said carefully, 'I have always known that Grandfather Will was German. When I was ten, my mother said she thought it was time I was told. She said it was a family secret and shouldn't ever be mentioned to anyone else. So I didn't. But Mother also said he was the finest man you could ever meet, he very wise and very kind, and they had all been guided by him. I didn't really think about him being German after that. It was only finding all these photographs and this funny notebook of our great grandmother, and this newspaper article.

Alice looked up at Margo. 'They must have been so worried.... I wonder why our grandmother kept it.'

'I didn't get it from Grandmother. Look at the photograph.'

Alice peered at the row of faded faces. 'Is one of them another relative?'

'Yes. On the very edge of the picture – can you see a man with wavy hair? That's the famous Gerard Belringer. His son gave it to me to show you.'

'Oh – do you mean Robert Belringer? The one Mark met? Who is only sort of related to us?'

'After Great Aunt Alice died, Gerard married her younger sister, our Great Aunt Emily. But... he did not marry Bo's mother when Bo came along some time later.'

'Oh? Oh I see! So ... so only a step-cousin really?

'I suppose so – even though his father was married to both our Great Aunts.'

'Isn't that amazing? So how old is Bo?'

'I think he is in his thirties so he must have been born sometime around 1930. What would Gerard Belringer have been then? Sixty perhaps? Great Aunt Emily was much younger so she was still alive when he was having an affair with Bo's mother. Bo says his mother said his father couldn't marry her because he wanted to be Mayor of Liverpool! Isn't that weird? Bo's mother is still alive. She was a district nurse and was awarded the MBE after the war.'

'Such complicated lives – and we knew nothing about any of them! There must be so many stories. I've got something to show you too, something that Robert sent me....'

Alice climbed off the bed and rummaged around in the bottom of her wardrobe 'Here. Mark told him I was interested in finding out about our family history and now he says he wants to help me do the research. Look – I think they are mainly more copies of old newspaper articles as well as some letters and legal documents. Lots of them are in German so I don't know what they mean. I've not had time to look at any of them properly or get them translated yet.'

Margo examined some of the articles. 'These must be from the First World War – Bo says his father worked with H.H. Asquith and the liberals then. But why he's kept German newspaper reports I wouldn't know. Perhaps he was a spy!'

'It's so funny to think we are all sort of related. How did you and Robert meet? Why do you call him Bo? It's an odd nick-name.'

'Robert Belringer become Bob Belringer – becomes Bo Jangles – you know the song?' Alice nodded vaguely. 'Bo says that he does sometimes feel that he has to sing and dance to entertain everyone! He's certainly got terrific charm. He came to talk to the children in my school about working in television, and everyone was wondering what all the noise was coming from my classroom!

'When he first heard my name, he realised we must have a family connection, so when we met up again, I showed him this old family album. He immediately found his father's wedding picture in it – to our Great Aunt Alice. He told me he had only ever had two photographs of his father – that newspaper cutting is one of them ...' Margo produced another photograph from her basket, '... and this was the other.'

Alice peered at it. 'But isn't that the same one as the picture in Grandmother's album?'

'Yes. But here you can see Gerard Belringer's face better. And he does look just like Bo.'

'I'm not sure if I ever actually saw him. You must show Mark later. He remembers him quite well.' She put the picture down.

'I do wonder why our great grandparents came to live here in the first place.'

'I don't know. Nobody ever talks about it. So many people still think that all Germans are Nazis.'

'I know. It's all those war films. Did any of our family join the army or navy during the war? I know Poppa didn't – I asked him once and he told me he'd twice gone along to join up but they'd turned him down because he had flat feet or something. I remember thinking at the time there was something funny about the way he said it.'

Margo said, 'No – none of them did. My mother says that my father was always terribly anxious. He worked at Catterick, where they were designing camouflage materials to hide air-fields and towns from the German bombers. I think Uncle Freddy was building Lancaster bombers. Edgar and Albert had their own garage business, so I suppose they might have been servicing army vehicles. I don't know what Philip or Clifford did.

'But during the First World War, all the older boys had to leave school and find work. They were stealing turnips from the fields for food sometimes. And they had a little sister who died in the diphtheria outbreak. It was such a sad awful time for them all. It all made my father desperately anxious and in some ways he's never stopped worrying – that's why it's so good to see him with your father now – laughing together.'

'Golly! I never knew anything about any of that. It's such a shame. I have never understood why Poppa never goes back to see his family, and this is the first time any of you have come to see us. We see all of Mum's family quite often. Do you think it's because of them being German?'

'Our parents were always great friends before your family moved away down south. Your mother came to stay and help my mother in the war when she was expecting my brother. I was christened after her. She is Hazel Margaret and I am Margaret Hazel. I think it is because your father has made lots of money and none of the others have....'

'Oh God! No! Poppa's not like that. The one thing he always has said is that your father was his favourite brother. It's just he doesn't seem to ever want to talk about the past. But he does say that your father taught him how to paint and what a wonderful artist he is. They still sometimes talk on the telephone, don't they? I'm sure I've heard them.''

'My father always wanted to be an architect. And he does paint beautifully. He still loves it.'

Alice pointed up to a small water-colour seascape hanging over the dressing table. 'That's one Pops painted during the war. But he doesn't seem to do it these days.'

'Your father was able to have a proper career after he left school. He was able to train for proper qualifications. My father says they couldn't afford for him to study to become an architect....'

'Well Pops really wanted to be a lawyer, but he wasn't able to because it would have taken too long and cost too much. He told me he only ever became an accountant because he hated watching his mother's struggles to bring up so many children, and he always vowed that his own wife would never have to do that. He had to work his socks off when he was young. He still does....'

'You know about Clifford, I suppose? The black sheep of the family?'

Alice shook her head.

'Oh well! He's the One We Don't Mention.'

'Why ever not! What did he do?'

Hazel's voice called up from downstairs, 'Alice! Margo! Lunch is ready!'

There was a sudden scampering sound and a sturdy black Scottie hurtled into the room and leapt straight onto the bed into Alice's lap, turning quickly round and staring curiously at Margo.

'MacBean! Have you come to get us?' Alice laughed and hugged him. 'I'd like to make a copy of all the letters and this wonderfully funny diary thing of Great-grandmother Anna's, Margo, if that's OK with you? I'll type it all out before you go. And you must tell me later about the one we don't mention. We'd better go down now.'

Sam and Leo were enjoying their reunion and when the two girls came downstairs Sam was regaling their visitors with one of his favourite stories.

'Oh not the parrot story, Poppa!' Alice exclaimed as she walked into the sitting room. Sam turned round to give her a defiant smile and to wave a greeting to Margo. Mark and Hazel raised their eyebrows in sympathetic despair with Alice, but

Leo and Martha both laughed and Leo said, 'No, no, please carry on Sam.'

'But it takes FOREVER!' Alice protested and Sam said 'I give up! I'm sure Margo never speaks to you like this does she, Leo?'

Leo smiled at Margo and said, 'I think daughters always have the upper hand as far as their fathers are concerned, Sam.'

'Well lunch is ready,' said Hazel. 'It's just fish pie because I want to watch the racing this afternoon.'

Over lunch Leo and Sam started talking about their boyhood days. Leo told them about Albert, their elder brother, who had gone to Africa for two years.

'Do you remember, Sam? He told us how he had gone on safari with a pal from work, and woken up in the middle of the night to see what he thought was a huge snake lying on his friend's chest? Albert had picked up his shotgun and fired it – only narrowly missing his pal, who sat up in terror, wearing pyjamas with a snake pattern on the front!'

Sam said, 'Albert was always doing crazy things. Do you remember the time when he thought he saw a rare bird through the window, and ran downstairs to get his camera, then back upstairs and put his head straight through the window – smashing the glass? He said...'

'... "But it was open a moment ago!"' Leo joined in. They both laughed affectionately at the memory.

Alice asked, 'Do you think either of you has changed much since you last saw each other?'

'Oh yes, Alice,' Leo answered at once. 'We are both far older and wiser than we were, aren't we Sam? But if you want to know what your father used to look like – look at your brother, Mark here. I got a shock when I first saw him, Sam. He is so like you as a young man.'

'Oh thank you very much!' said Mark. 'I'm not a bald old coot!'

'Ah you just wait, young man! When you've seen as much of life as we have you'll be glad to have any hair left at all you can call your own!'

Hazel said, 'Clear the plates away please, Alice, and bring in the cheese board – if anyone would like some? We'll have our coffee in the sitting room.'

'Mum wants to get to her racing on television,' Mark explained to Leo and Martha. 'We always have to gobble down our Saturday lunch!'

'Oh! Do you like to gamble on the horses, Hazel?' Martha asked. Mark and Sam looked up to the heavens as Hazel started to say, 'No, no. It's just...'

'... just enough to keep her bookies living in the comfort they have grown accustomed to!' said Sam.

'Oh really, Sam!' said Hazel crossly. 'You are a liar! I just have a few very small bets for fun on a Saturday afternoon.'

Alice came back in with a cheese-board and put it on the table. She said, 'Why have you never told us anything about our family history, Poppa?'

Sam said with a little laugh, 'There's nothing of interest to tell. Most of the time life was just a hard struggle for us all. You don't want to hear about all that.'

'But, Dad, they are our family....'

'There were many sad things, Alice. That's all over, thank heavens. Don't jog backwards.' He lit a cigarette. 'Now let's talk about something more cheerful.'

'Well, what about The One We Don't Mention, Poppa? Which one was he?'

A look of pain crossed Sam's face, but Leo was laughing, 'Oh so Margo's been telling you about our Clifford, has she? Our brother Clifford went to live in Australia after the war, Alice, and I don't think any of us has heard from him since.'

Mark said, 'So why is he called The One We Don't Mention? Whatever did he do?'

Leo glanced at Sam and then said, 'Clifford was always getting himself into trouble as a young man. Clifford wasn't a bad sort really. He was just a bit of rebel who was led astray.'

'I bet I would have liked him!'

'I expect you would, Alice. I hear you are a bit of a rebel yourself. And Clifford certainly had charm. But someone I think you would have loved even more was your grandfather. Now there was a wise, kindly man. He was always smiling and had those warm twinkling eyes – and I think in his own way he was a great man.'

Leo looked at Sam, who nodded in slow agreement. Leo went on, 'But even so, your father and I and all our brothers had to grow up very quickly when we were boys, Alice, and we had to learn some very hard lessons about the world. We did tell Margo and our own boys about our German connection, but it was something that caused us all so much pain, we have always preferred not to talk any more about it. But perhaps, Sam...' he turned to his brother, 'it's time to tell the younger generation a little more about how things were? So they can understand?'

'I hope they never have to,' Sam said.

Leo nodded thoughtfully, 'Perhaps you are right.'

'There are some things it's far better not to know.'

While their parents went through into the sitting room with the coffee, Mark, Alice and Martha went out into the kitchen to do the washing up.

Mark said sternly, 'It's a man's work, washing-up! Alice never does it properly. I'll wash and you girls can dry.' He began running hot water into the sink, then tying on an apron and ostentatiously pulling on yellow rubber gloves while Alice and Margo both laughed at him.

'Well in that case, I'll put away and Margo can dry your perfect handiwork.'

Alice went out with the trolley, and came back with the glasses and cheese plates, closely followed by an intensely interested MacBean, keeping his eyes fixed on the bottom tray. 'Don't be silly, MacBean. You know you aren't allowed.'

Alice went out again to finish clearing the rest of the things off the table while Mark and Margo began washing and drying the glasses.

'Tell us more about this mysterious Uncle Clifford,' Mark said. 'The One We Don't Mention. Whatever had he done?'

'I don't know really. I think he may have stolen some money from his work. It was during the war and I think he was sent to prison for a bit, and then went off to live in Australia. It's almost a family joke now – The One We Don't Mention – but our grandmother Leah was very upset and didn't want it ever talked about. She and our grandfather were very serious, mor-al-minded people, as I expect you know. Were you brought up in Christian Science?'

'No. Oh yes – of course! I had forgotten all about that. We used to laugh when Pa said he had been brought up in Christian Science, because nobody likes to discuss his symptoms with his doctor more than he does! I think he gave up Christian Science years ago.... Were you?'

'Yes. My brothers and I are still members.'

'Really? Neither of our parents are at all religious ... are they, Al?' Alice had come back into the kitchen and was putting the dry plates and glasses away.

'No.' she agreed. 'Mum says that when her father was alive they all had to go to Methodist Sunday school three times every Sunday, and that was enough to last her a life-time. Neither of them has been confirmed – and Pops hasn't even been baptised. We only ever go to church on Christmas day. Pops doesn't come even then.'

'Al and I would probably never even have been christened ourselves if I hadn't gone to Rugby. When I was fourteen, the chaplain asked me for my "baptismal certificate". I had no idea what he was talking about. He said I needed it because all the boys in my year were going to be confirmed during the next term. I wrote and told Ma, and she arranged for Al and me both to be christened in the local church during the holidays.'

'Yes, I was ten,' Alice agreed. 'I had no idea why we were doing it.'

'The chaplain at Rugby was a great guy. He was a war hero and only had one leg and we all admired him. I went through a sort of 'religious' phase while he was preparing us for confirmation. I even went along to a Christian Science meeting one evening, just out of curiosity to see what it was like. There was some completely dotty woman saying that her car had fallen in the ditch and the chauffeur had been very upset but she had just touched it with one hand, and he had been able to drive it out! So that put me off for ever!'

'Oh dear! Yes, you do get some odd-balls. I rarely go to testimony meetings myself now, but I do know lots of people that it has helped. But Christian Science isn't really a religion – it's more a philosophy, or a way of life. And some quite famous people follow its ideas. We are not taught that God is a mysterious invisible magic person sitting on a cloud, but Principle, Mind, Soul, Spirit, Life, Truth and Love. If you follow those principles it helps you to live a good life.'

'But doesn't it say that if you fall ill it's because you have been wicked or are morally unsound or something?'

'No! The idea is simply that if you have a truthful, positive, courageous attitude to life, you will keep physically healthy.'

Mark turned round from the sink and winked at her. 'Goodness! I never knew I was doing all that – but I am very healthy!'

Alice said, 'Actually, I think Poppa does pretty much think like that. I mean, I know he likes going to see the doctor and all that, but he's full of wise sayings about how to live a good life, isn't he? But he always says that Shakespeare is his Bible.'

Mark carefully pulled off his rubber washing up gloves and untied the apron. 'I call him Polonius!'

They all laughed.

'Well now that's done – I'm off to play a few rounds of golf with Dickie. Why don't you and Margo take poor old MacBean out for a walk, Alice? He's looking very fed up.'

'Let's go into the garden and enjoy a smoke.' Sam and Leo had finished their coffee just as Hazel was turning on the television and reaching for her newspaper.

The two men went outside and paused to look back in through the window at their two wives sitting together in front of the television set. Leo laughed.

'This will be a new experience for Martha!'

They could see Martha was saying something to Hazel, who was nodding vaguely, her eyes glued to the screen. Her hand was reaching out for the telephone beside her chair.

The two men walked on down the garden and sat down on a bench beside the large lily pond at the bottom. Sam had provided them each with a cigar.

'What a beautiful place you live in, Sam!'

'Yes. We love it here.'

They lit their cigars and sat in thoughtful silence for awhile.

'Talking about the family with Alice has made me think, Sam. You don't happen to know whatever became of Gerard Belringer, do you? Margo has recently made friends with a son of his, Robert, who I believe young Mark has met too, and Margo says that Robert never saw his father again once the war started. I hadn't thought about Gerard for years, and certainly didn't know that he had a son, but I remember you and he used to be good friends. I thought you might know.'

'He came to visit us a few times when we first moved down to Richmond. The first time, he was on his way to Germany, and he asked if he would mind if he brought us a young German woman back with him to stay for a few months until he could find her somewhere to live over here, because things were so difficult, especially in East Berlin. We were happy to help of course. After that he brought us three different girls.

They only ever stayed for a few months, helping Hazel with the children and taking English speaking classes.'

'What I wondered was, did he ever discover what had become of his daughter, Maisie?'

'I don't know. He never talked about it. He also never mentioned having a son. I had no idea. After a couple of years he stopped appearing, and then we never heard from him again. He simply vanished as far as we were concerned. So I don't know if he ever found out what happened to poor Maisie.'

Leo shook his head, 'Very sad.'

'My one aim in life has been to make life different for Mark and Alice. I want my children to look forwards, not back. I never wanted Hazel to go through what our mother had to...'

'Well you have certainly succeeded in doing that, Sam. I can see how much you must both love living here.'

'Yes.... It's a long way back to Manchester.'

Vergissmeinnicht

Scotland – March 2016

I did meet Robert Belringer, 'Bo', back in the sixties. and we talked about the project enthusiastically for over a year. Margo and I also had many conversations about it. But after a while my enthusiasm began to wane. I knew my father didn't want to talk or even think about the past, and so I thought I should wait. Then I became busy with living my own life. So I didn't write it in the sixties ... or in the seventies ... or in the eighties ... or the nineties....

Then, about fifteen years ago, my eldest grandson, James, then aged eleven, told me he was 'doing' World War Two for history at his school. I suddenly realised that I had never told him any of this. I said carefully, 'Your great-great-*great* grand-father was German.'

'Yuk!' James said at once. Adding more hopefully after a moment, 'is the blood dead yet?'

Even now! He hated the idea of being German and didn't want to know anything about it.

It had come as quite a shock to realise that a period of time that I had lived through was on the secondary school history syllabus. I wondered how they would have felt, Otto and Anna, those citizens of the world, if they had known that most of their grandchildren and great-great grandchildren wouldn't be told where they came from, that their descendants would never know anything about them ... or that a great-great-great grandchild of theirs would one day say only, 'Yuk!'

I've always kept copies of all the old notebooks and one or two copies of the photographs Mark had shown me years before. It was now or never.

My partner, Charlie, and I began by going to the Isle of Man. There's nothing much left to see of the old camp at Knockaloe, which must have been dismantled years ago, but there is a small graveyard where the graves of the prisoners who died there can be seen. At Ramsey you could still see signs along the sea-front where the barricades and barbed wire had been fixed. In the museum there are records of the names of hundreds of the internees from both world wars, Otto's and William's among them. There are even a few photographs of the prisoners at Knockaloe and one of the men in the orchestra they managed to form.

Charlie and I went to Berlin. So much of West Berlin appears much as it would have looked in the nineteenth century, everything seems to have been rebuilt in the same classical style. It is possible to visualise how it must have looked before the First World War, and much harder to realise that it was all in ruins in 1945.

The east side of Berlin is another story. In the 19th century Anna Ackermann's family home stood in Berlin Stadt, a hundred yards down the road from her father, Emil's, silk and velvet factory. Nearby was a great military church, Gnaden-Invalidenkirche, with its own hospital for soldiers and their families. House, factory, church and hospital no longer exist. They were all destroyed by Allied bombs during World War 2, and all signs of their existence were completely cleared away by the Stasi; it is now a large, bare, concrete space, foreground to some featureless blocks of post-war flats.

Across the road, beside the last remnants of the Berlin Wall – which didn't exist then, and doesn't exist now – the old military grave-yard is still there, with the headstones of soldiers and their family of two centuries leaning about under tall trees in grassy woodland, including one engraved with the names of *Baron Leopold General von Treitschke* and *General Hermann von Treitschke.* In another part of the graveyard we found the graves of Hans and Shirley Schindler.

I even managed to uncover the great secret that only Gerard knew, and never told Maisie. The old *Gnaden-Invaliden* registry of births, marriages and deaths still exists and includes the following entries:

19 November 1872: *Anna Ackermann, daughter of Emil von Ackermann, velvet and silk merchant, married Otto Lohmann, Klavierstimmer.*

1 April 1873: *In Invaliden hospital: to Anna Lohmann, a daughter.*

Margarethe must have been that daughter, born only 5 months after Anna's and Otto's wedding, and then, I assume, adopted by Anna's sister, Liese. I am certain that she must have been General Hermann von Treitschke's daughter.

*

They didn't leave much of a record – a few old photographs, one or two letters, Anna's funny note-book, So I have only been able to imagine how it might have been. For over ten years after James' 'Yuk!' I was struggling to put it all together – at least a version of their story – and was wondering if I'd ever be able to finish it.

Then one day I was standing in my kitchen warming my backside against the Aga, thinking about them all and suddenly – there he was, in my kitchen, silently smiling and nodding with his twinkling brown eyes – my Grandfather Wilhelm – straight out of the pictures in the old photograph album that

Mark showed me all those years ago. Then my Great-grandfather Otto was here too, and Great-grandmother Anna, sitting at my kitchen table; and Great-uncle Freddie. A young Gerard Belringer was laughing. Tall Hans came in and had to stoop low under the doorway, because he had 5-year-old Maisie on his shoulders. The room was filling up with smiling black and white ghosts from the old family album, waiting for something to happen, the party to begin. My own parents, Sam and Hazel, appeared – younger and happier than I can ever remember seeing them.

Then my old donkey, much loved but also long dead, tried to push his way in through the glass door from the garden into my crowded kitchen, and I said, 'Stop!' and everyone vanished.

I've finished it now. I didn't forget you. I've opened the champagne – I do hope that's why you came.

Alice Lohmann
Scotland – March, 2016

Acknowledgements

I owe so many thanks to my great friend, Judith Stevenson, who gave me huge amounts of encouragement and *helpful* much needed criticism during our weekly lunches. And thanks, too, to Rose Pipes, who as a favour became a stern and exacting copy-editor, who took her task so seriously she even taught me the difference between a dash and hyphen, and counted all my dots.... My cousin Margaret urged me on when she thought I was back-sliding; Geoffrey Stevenson generously took on the task of helping me to get it all ready for self-publishing with Lulu. Without all of them I wouldn't have finished yet.

Above all, I want to thank my dearest Andrew, whose support, along with his amazing collection of old magazines, maps, newspapers and books furnished 90% of the research – who needs Google when you've got a husband who never throws anything away?

Thank you to all of them, with all my heart.

#0042 - 180416 - C0 - 210/148/17 - PB - DID1427587